WHO i was supposed to Be

SHORT STORIES

SUSAN PERABO

SIMON & SCHUSTER

SIMON & SCHUSTER
Rockefeller Center
1230 Avenue of the Americas
New York, NY 10020

SIMON & SCHUSTER and colophon are registered trademarks of Simon & Schuster Inc.

Designed by Karolina Harris
Manufactured in the United States of America
1 2 3 4 5 6 7 8 9 10

Library of Congress Cataloging-in-Publication Data
Perabo, Susan, [date]
Who I was supposed to be : short stories / Susan Perabo.
p. cm.
1. United States—Social life and customs—20th century—Fiction. I. Title.
PS3566.E673W48   1999
813'.54—DC21   99-12256
CIP
Rev.
ISBN 0-684-86233-6

"Thick as Thieves" previously appeared in Story. "The Greater Grace of Carlisle" previously appeared in Glimmer Train. "Explaining Death to the Dog" previously appeared in The Missouri Review and New Stories from the South. "Who I Was Supposed to Be" previously appeared in Black Warrior Review. "Gravity" previously appeared in Indiana Review and New Stories from the South. "The Rocks Over Kyburz" previously appeared in Denver Quarterly. "Some Say the World" previously appeared in TriQuarterly, New Stories from the South, and Best American Short Stories 1996.

ACKNOWLEDGMENTS

I'D first like to thank my editor at Simon & Schuster, Marysue Rucci, for her extraordinary work and support; I couldn't have dreamed up a better editor. Also thanks to David Rosenthal and the countless people at S&S who have helped along the way. I am extremely grateful to my agent, Elyse Cheney of Sanford J. Greenburger Associates, for her hard work, contagious excitement, and mind-numbing speed. I'd like to thank the folks at Dickinson College for giving me the opportunity to live the double life of teacher/writer with as much ease as is possible, and also my students, who teach me more than I teach them and are a constant source of joy and inspiration. I'd like to thank the entire faculty of the University of Arkansas M.F.A. program (most especially Jim Whitehead, Skip Hays, Joanne Meschery, Bill Harrison, and Brian Wilkie, honorary member), who turned me from some pretty shaky raw material into a writer, a teacher, and a reader of great books. They read many of the stories in this collection with a care and wisdom a writer should expect only from her dearest friends, and for that I am eternally grateful to The Program. Special thanks for friendship, support, and brutal honesty from the guys of the Fayetteville writing group that has continued long past Fayetteville: David Prattmania, Steven Shay

Yates, Sidney "PC" Thompson, Jay Skippah Prefontaine, Randolph "Lord Walnut Bowls" Thomas, and the man who reads everything I write, Bradford "Famous Guy" Barkley. Thanks finally and most especially to Mom, Dad, Betsy, and Sha'an, for help on and off the page, and way too much to capture in a few simple words.

*This book is dedicated to the late great Betty Broeder Feldmann.
In March of '93 she pointed at me and said, "Sue, are you
writing all this down?" Typically, it was as much a directive as a
question. I keep telling her, even now, "Hey, I'm trying."*

CONTENTS

"For, while the tale of how we suffer, and how we are delighted, and how we may triumph is never new, it always must be heard. There isn't any other tale to tell, it's the only light we've got in all this darkness."

JAMES BALDWIN,
"Sonny's Blues"

THICK AS THIEVES

i

A M   fifty-nine, and I did not make the graceful transition
into late middle age so vital for a Hollywood actor; instead of
stocky I grew fat, my chiseled nose and chin softened from
unique to ugly. One glorious morning I looked in the mirror and
saw the coveted "distinguished." The next morning, when I
looked again, I was simply old.

Of course, if I chose to write a tell-all extravaganza I could
quite probably bring myself back into the limelight for a few
frenzied moments. But I have no desire to write such a book. I
have only one worthwhile story to tell, and it is neither about
sex, booze, exotic locales, nor the grossly overrated Golden Age
of Hollywood. It is instead about my father, who died this past
March at eighty-one.

I was a poor son to my father. A heart attack claimed my
mother at the startling age of thirty-one; I was nine years old,
and my father was left with the puzzling task of raising a son
alone. At seventeen I left him—for all practical purposes—
childless. I fled west on the back of a touring company bus to
pursue acting, and saw him perhaps a dozen times in the subse-
quent thirty years. He managed a supermarket in Bangor,
Maine, until he was seventy-six. A few years later he was put

in a retirement home by his sister Sara, who died shortly thereafter.

By the time all of this had transpired, I was living in Los Angeles with my fourth wife and her two nearly grown children, who often listened to Tchaikovsky's *1812 Overture* at full volume while snorting cocaine off their mother's family heirlooms. It had been eight years since my last Oscar nomination (supporting actor, which I lost to a boy of fourteen), and I was starting to see a pattern in the few scripts that were sent to my agent: the crusty old father, the crusty old boss, the crusty old teacher. My wife was an actress as well, but she was far from crusty. She was forty-one, she was on television, and she did step aerobics with her private trainer in our living room at 7:00 A.M. while I slept, thanks only to the miracle of earplugs. Often when I woke there was a brief and happy moment when I could not remember her name. Such was our life together, which lasted a very long three years.

I was beginning to feel like a failure then, in the waning days of love and fame. I could not seem to get it straight how to live with someone, bungled through each relationship like a cow trying to piece together an intricate model of the PT 109 with its cumbersome hooves. I thought of my parents' marriage, which, whether from great devotion or simply lack of time, never soured, at least not that I knew of. My father had some secret, I thought, and I had never taken advantage of his wisdom.

And so, a year ago September, I phoned him in Maine and asked him to come to Los Angeles.

"I'll pay of course," I said.

"Who the hell is this?" my father said. "Fred? Is this a prank?"

My wife was going to Paris to do a TV movie, some steamy number revolving around lovers, drugs, and murder. Perhaps this was the actual title; I do not know. Regardless, she planned to take her delinquents with her, and I suspected that she and I might never sleep in the same bed again, because the morning they were to leave she jarred me awake as the sun was coming up.

"Jack. Jack!" She slapped furiously at her pillow.

"What is it?" I asked, alarmed.

"People think we're in love!" she shouted, loudly enough to prompt the collie next door into fits of barking. "Isn't that a riot?"

"Lower your voice," I said. "It's—"

"I feel *empty*." She flung the covers on top of me and sat there stiffly, her tanned and muscular legs stretched out before her like trophies. "You *make* me feel empty, Jack."

Her name was Lorraine. Downstairs, something shattered. We had twenty-four rooms in our home, eleven paintings worth over forty thousand dollars apiece, seven cars, and three machines to grind coffee beans. My life, I thought while lying there looking at the wife's legs, had been reduced to numbers across a spreadsheet, a tally. Twenty-four plus eleven plus seven plus three plus two stunningly young legs. Plus fifty-nine.

My father arrived that afternoon in a taxi. He carried a thick plaid bag, wore blue slacks and an untucked white shirt, sneakers, a gray windbreaker, and a hat. My father was a well-built man, fit but short; my mother had been tall, and in pictures I have seen of them he is always wearing a hat, the top of which reaches just to her forehead.

"Jack." He put out his hand, worn as an old glove, still chapped from years of packing freezers. He was eighty and his face was round and white, lips thin. His hair was exactly the color of his windbreaker, a light gray like storm clouds, two shades lighter than it had been when I last saw him, five years before.

"Hi Dad." I turned around, gestured to the house. "What'dya think?"

He nodded, took it all in. A part of me wanted him to faint dead away: I the son with the mansion, he the father in the old hat.

"A nice spread." He took a pair of thick glasses from his windbreaker pocket, put them on and squinted at the house. "You have a wife?"

"Yes," I said. "But she's away."

"For good?" He switched the suitcase to his other hand.

"On vacation."

"Uh huh." He nodded knowingly. I imagined him reading about me in magazines, following my fictional life through old articles and pictures of me with a woman on my arm and a drink in my hand.

I took him to a room upstairs, two down from Lorraine's and mine. He had a view of the neighborhood, and, for his wrinkled old clothes, an antique mahogany dresser with brass knobs that I had bought at an auction for four thousand dollars. He sat down on the bed with a huff and held the suitcase on his lap.

"You in a movie now?" he asked.

"No. I'm between projects."

"You look good. You don't look sixty."

I straightened my shoulders, picked a fuzz ball off my sweater. "I'm not."

He removed his hat and set it carefully beside him on the bed as if it were made of glass. "I saw you on the television last week," he said. "On the oldies channel. Edna Burnside, she's got an apartment down from mine, said you were one of her favorites. I told her you were my son and she didn't believe me."

He was able to say this without a hint of resentment, and I gave him credit for that, whether it was acting or not.

"I'll come for a visit," I said. "I suspect that would show her."

"I guess so." But he didn't sound very enthusiastic. Perhaps he didn't believe I would ever come; perhaps he could hear truth in my voice that, after years of performing, I could no longer discern.

Later we sat in the living room and watched the Dodgers lose to the Giants. I was already regretting having asked him to come; now that he had arrived I didn't know what to say. He apparently did not, as I had hoped, have a fatherly sixth sense that provoked him to answer questions without my having to ask them. I sup-pose I had imagined he would take one long knowing look at me and then, in no uncertain terms, tell me how to fix my life. But instead he drank his beer and made small talk about the game, and I did not know how to reach him without sounding like a fool. So I kept quiet, sipped at my scotch and imagined the phone ringing, a familiar voice on the other end saying: "Jack, we were all sitting here wondering what you were up to . . ." but I could think of no one who would make such a call.

"Hey Jack?"

I looked up.

"Time for my medicine," my father said. "I want to catch the end of the game, but I've got to take the pills on time. Would you run upstairs and get 'em for the old man?"

"Sure." I set my scotch down, stood up.

"Jack?"

"Yeah?"

"They're on the outside compartment, the one with the snaps. The snaps. You got it? On the outside."

I nodded, climbed the stairs to his room and took his suitcase from on top of the dresser and set it on the bed. I unsnapped the compartment and found three bottles of medication: ibuprofen, Elavil, something that sounded like a planet in a science fiction picture: Zestril. Then I flipped the suitcase open and looked at my father's things. He had three pairs of pants that were exactly the same, brand-new boxer shorts, red swimming trunks. I pushed the clothes aside. Under them were magazines—Newsweek, People, California Living—and a small black leather bag, the kind I had seen tied around the waists of the skateboarding terrors in the neighborhood. I picked it up, heard loose change chattering inside. I turned to the doorway, made sure I was still alone. I imagined he was dead, that I was sorting through his possessions, trying to unravel his life. I unzipped the bag. Inside were two of Lorraine's diamond bracelets, the string of pearls I had given her for our first anniversary, and about forty pennies.

"Jack?" my father called. I could tell he was at the foot of the stairs. "I gotta take those pills on time, Jack."

I went into the hallway, stood at the top of the staircase and held up the bag. His foot was on the first step, his hand wrapped around the banister. He squinted.

"Those my pills?"

"No."

He walked slowly up the stairs, not taking his eyes off mine. When he reached the top he took the bag from my grasp.

"I get off schedule on those pills I'm six feet under," he said. He brushed past me and went into his room.

"What's going on here?" I turned just in time to see him put the pack back into his suitcase.

"Arthritis, insomnia, high BP."

"Why didn't you tell me you needed money?"

"What the hell are you talking about?" He popped the pills into his mouth, swallowed them dry. "Death narrowly averted for another day." He sighed.

"You've stolen from me," I said.

"What?"

"You sent me up here to find that stuff? Didn't you?"

He broke into a tremendous smile. "God, I tried, Jack," he said, grinning like a groomsman. "I tried so hard. But I was just aching to tell someone. And seeing if I still knew you as well as I thought I did, you little sneak. I'm proud of you, sniffing through your old man's things."

"Don't turn this around. You stole my jewelry."

"This stuff yours? You one of those?"

"It's my wife's. It's the same thing."

"Not with you it's not. Not from what I hear."

I spun around, fully intending to stomp out of the room like a four-year-old, and saw his bathrobe hanging on the back of the door, something black sticking out of the pocket. I yanked it out—a black ski mask. I turned it over in my hands, ran my thumbs along the rough wool. It reminded me of a hat I had worn when I was a boy, walking to school on snowy dark Maine mornings, and I could feel the hot breath coming back onto my lips, the wool stuck to my tongue, as distinctly as if I had worn such a mask that morning and not thousands of mornings ago.

"You're good, Jack," my father said. "You got the part down.

You know just where to look for the clues." He took the ski mask from me and pulled it down over his face. "Pretty spooky, eh?"

"Cut it out," I said.

"What's that?" His voice, muffled.

"Take it off," I said. "Come on."

He pulled it up to his eyebrows, smiled at me. "It's just for show, anyway," he said. "I can't really wear it. Blocks my peripheral vision."

"What do you need peripheral vision for?" I asked warily.

He clasped his hands together. "Have you ever stolen around in the night, Jack? I don't mean with women. You, alone, listening to the hammer of your heart."

I just stared at him, unable to form any kind of answer to such a question.

"Well have you?"

I shook my head. "I've never taken things from anybody, if that's what you mean."

"It's not about the *things*," he said. "It's about the taking. The thrill." He stood up, went to the window and put his hands against the glass. "The purest thrill you'd ever know, Jack."

I steadied myself in the doorway. "You've done this before?"

He turned. "Hell, sure," he said. "But just small time. I thought I'd come out here and expand my horizons. I've been reading up—I'm ready for a serious heist."

I took a step toward him. "You're kidding me."

"Why would I?"

I sunk down on the bed. "What do you do with it?"

"Give it away," he said.

"To whom?"

"As presents," he said. "I wrap the jewelry and give it out to the ladies I live with. They bake me cookies, I give them jewelry. What a thrill, Jack, to give somebody such a gift. But that's secondary."

"But why steal?"

"I'm retired," he said, smiling. "I have nothing else to do."

"What about stamp collecting?"

His smile faded. "What do you think I am, Jack?" he asked. "Some dying old coot? All my life I've been piddling around. This is it, the end of the piddling."

"But it doesn't make any sense."

"It makes perfect sense. You don't understand because your whole life has been exciting. You get to put on costumes every day, do crazy things. This"—he touched his ski mask—"is the first costume I've ever gotten to wear. But it's better than what you do. It's the real thing."

"You're a kleptomaniac."

"Wrong," he said proudly. "I'm an *actor*. Guess I just wanted to show off a little bit. I thought of bungling the crime but I couldn't do it, no matter how hard I tried. I'm too good, Jack. But I hadda tell you."

"I don't even know who you are," I said.

He straightened himself, smirked. "I'm anybody I want to be."

I had known him only once, I decided that night, known him the summer before I left home, when I worked as a bag boy at his supermarket. And I knew him then through watching him work. My father would do anything to get customers into his store, even to get people into his parking lot. That summer I played gofer for him when I wasn't bagging; he apparently assumed I would do anything because I was his son. One Saturday we dressed up in chicken costumes, my father and I, and played badminton in the parking lot.

"People will come to see," he said. "They'll get into the lot, realize it's just a couple chickens playing badminton, and then remember they need to pick up a loaf of bread."

Sadly, he was right; the ploy worked, causing me to undergo many more Saturdays of humiliation, including the worst one, raffle day, when I stood in front of the store under a sign that read WIN ME and was the free dinner date for the lucky ticket holder, a ticket going for just ten dollars' worth of groceries.

But my father, for all his ridiculous notions, ran the store with an efficiency unequaled by any director I have ever worked with. On days when I did not have to perform stunts and just bagged groceries, my father would send me after foods that customers had forgotten. "Aisle seven, twelve steps down, on the bottom," he'd call after me. Or: "Sixth freezer, aisle three." And he knew the people too, although it was not some small town grocery with the same hundred customers each week. It was a chain, strangers in and out a thousand times a day. But not one, it seemed, was a stranger to my father. Some of the customers would seek him out among the aisles, tell him the news of their lives, as if he were their father and not mine.

In the morning we walked. I couldn't recall the last time I had walked for any reason other than getting somewhere, but my father said if he missed his morning stroll his blood pressure might skyrocket, and I was wary of letting him out of my sight. He mentioned nothing of the night before, though, and so I allowed myself to believe that sometime in the middle of the night his senses had gotten the better of him and all craziness was over.

He was clearly impressed by the neighborhood. At the foot of each lawn he paused on the sidewalk, gazed up at the house, and whistled low under his breath.

"Fantasyland," he said each time.

At the corner we came upon the Hacketts' house, and discovered Marilyn Hackett playing lawn croquet in her nightgown while her husband Frank sat in a wooden rocker in the middle of the lawn sipping on a cup of coffee and reading *Variety*.

"What's this spectacle?" my father asked.

Before I had a chance to answer, or flee, Marilyn spotted us midswing and shouted, "Look who it is!" for the whole neighborhood to hear. "Look, Frank! It's Jack!"

I hadn't seen the Hacketts in months. Frank was a producer and Marilyn, as far as I had been able to tell, made her living laughing. She laughed at parties and premieres and weddings and wakes with equal force, while Frank stood by with the bemused look of an overindulgent father whose child has just wet her pants in a crowded elevator. I gave a quick wave and was already turning back in the direction of my house when my father shouted, "There is nothing more *exquisite* than a woman playing croquet in her *nightgown!*"

This pleased Marilyn Hackett to no end. She came galloping barefoot down the lawn and reached us, breathless, her croquet mallet over her shoulder.

"Who's this, Jack?"

I introduced her to my father, who took the mallet from her shoulder and putted a pebble at his feet. "It's all in the elbows," he told Marilyn.

I looked up the lawn at Frank Hackett, who was eyeing us over his paper, and was stung by a chilling thought: a job, I realized, was just one well-placed ass kiss away. If my father charmed the Hacketts, it was not impossible to think that my agent would receive a phone call the following morning. I swallowed my self-revulsion and called, "How're things, Frank?" prompting him to set down his paper and join us on the sidewalk. He extended his hand for me to admire, then shake.

"Long time, et cetera," he said.

"I've been Bangor Maine croquet champ for twelve years running," my father announced. "Last year they asked me to throw a match." He nudged Marilyn. "Said I was discouraging young talent."

Marilyn Hackett howled at this, a statement I assumed was an outright lie.

"What're you working on these days?" I asked Frank.

He ignored me, turned to my father. "People don't play croquet anymore," he said, as indignant as if he had invented the game himself. "Every blowhard in this town walks his fat ass around eighteen holes and thinks of himself as a gentleman because he uses a putter instead of a mallet."

"True indeed, Franklin," my father said, clapping him on the shoulder. "However I suspect this lady could pique some interest in the sport." My father winked at Marilyn. "Especially with the lingerie angle."

Marilyn blushed, although her nightgown, a purple tentlike affair, hardly qualified as lingerie.

"Say," my father added. "I'm not sure I can hold off on draining the radiator till we get back to Jack's place. Could you point me to your little boy's room?"

Frank turned back to his castle, considering. It was a crude request in such a neighborhood, the use of another's toilet.

"It's not very—" I started.

"Through the front hall on your right," Marilyn interrupted.

My father took a few steps. "Not going to set off one of those newfangled alarms, am I?"

"Not unless you open a safe!" Marilyn hooted.

I watched my father ascend the lawn and open the front door. He stepped into the front hall and glanced over his shoulder. Frank and Marilyn had their backs to him; he gave me a quick nod and went to the left.

"Anybody catch that ball game last night?" I asked, my voice barely a squeak.

Marilyn grasped my arm ecstatically. "Why didn't you tell us you had a father, Jack?"

"Everyone has a father," Frank said.

Marilyn ignored him. "He's an absolute riot. You'll have to make the rounds with that one."

I nodded, half listening, half wondering what room my father was presently creeping through, what treasures his rough hands were falling upon.

"Let's see it," I said, as we walked home. After my father had returned from his adventure in the house we had spent another exhausting half hour on the Hacketts' lawn, my father entertaining Marilyn with hilarious tales from the grocery business while sweat dripped down my back.

"See what?" he asked.

"Dad. Come on."

He grinned, patted the pocket of his windbreaker.

Thanks to the Hacketts, my father became the toast of the town that week; I got more invitations for drinks than I had received in months. The secret: Hollywood people, especially old Hollywood people, are starved for outsiders. Anything non-Hollywood is refreshing; the fact that my father was entertaining to boot was only a plus. And so we visited, and ripped off, three more neighbors, and never heard a word about anything being stolen, never saw a police car.

"They don't even *miss* it," my father said over lunch one afternoon. He pointed his fork at me. "This is the truly amazing part, Jack."

"They miss it," I said. "It's just not worth the trouble, probably."

"I enjoy their company," he said, shaking his head. "But I'll never understand how it's not worth the trouble."

"Because you're not rich," I said.

"I don't have one ounce of desire to be rich," he said. "Those people who live behind you, what're their names?"

"The Gundersons?"

"Did you know that every day they drive a different car? Every morning I sit on the deck and goddamnit if every morning they don't coast out of that garage with a brand-new automobile."

"I doubt they're all brand-new," I said. "Besides, what do you care if—"

"I'm tired of that silly old man role," he interrupted, angrily throwing his napkin onto the table. "I'm tired of acting like an old fool just so I can lift a piece of jewelry nobody even misses."

"Then stop."

"I will." He said it with resolution, with surprise, as if the thought had never before occurred to him. He got up from the table and marched up to his room. I did not see him for the rest of the afternoon.

•

That night while rinsing the dinner dishes my father announced he was going to rob the Gundersons.

"You said you were quitting," I protested.

"I most certainly did not." He turned off the water in the sink, handed me a rinsed salad bowl. "You didn't listen. I said I was quitting the old man role."

I loaded the bowl into the dishwasher and kicked the door closed. "Dad . . ." I said, trying to keep myself from shouting. "Dad, I hate to break it to you, but it's not a role."

He grinned. "You tell me that after I bust in there and clean them out."

"What do you mean, bust in?" I asked. "Are you crazy? You can't break into their house."

"I've done this before, Jack." He lit his pipe and leaned against the counter.

"Not this part," I said. "This isn't Shady Hills Old Folks Home, you know. It's one thing to bullshit people, but you can't just waltz in somewhere in the middle of the night. This is Los Angeles. People have burglar alarms. People have *guns*, Dad."

"Oak Hills," he said.

"What?"

He scowled at me through the fog of smoke. "Not Shady Hills goddamn Old Folks Home. Oak Hills Retirement Community."

"Whatever," I said.

"I'm telling you I've done research, Jack. *Extensive research.* You wouldn't believe the stuff they put in magazines these days." He shook his head. "It's scary thinking of kids out there getting their hands on some of this reading material."

"It's not the kids I'm worried about," I said.

"Don't worry about *me*, Jack. I'm telling you I know what I'm doing."

I took some bourbon from the pantry, poured a shot into a nearby coffee mug. "Listen, things happen," I said softly, staring down into the mug. "People get a little crazy sometimes and it doesn't help to have crappy children."

"You're not a crappy child," my father said. "Look at this, big house, swimming pool."

"You know what I mean. If it's something I've done, some way I've instigated this. . . ."

"You know, Jack," he said, puffing away, "you always gave yourself too much credit. This doesn't have one rat's ass to do with you. I made my own choices, Jack. Your mother taught me how to do that."

"You're going to get caught. You're not built for this, Dad, I'm telling you."

"You come with me and see," he said.

I scoffed, threw back my drink. "Then we'll both get caught."

"Remember that one movie," he said. "Your brother got waxed by the mob—what'd he get, shot?"

I poured myself another drink. "Drowned."

"Right, the cement, and you had to avenge him. You wore that cool hat over your eyes and blew smoke rings and made all the right moves. You were perfect."

"This isn't a movie."

"That's my point," he said. "You weren't really that guy. But you wanted to be, didn't you? Just a little part of you?"

"You can't just go around being everybody you want to be."

"You pick and choose," he said. "You pick the roles that suit you. Your role is to sit around this big house feeling sorry for your sorry life. I choose something a little more inspiring." He took a final puff off his pipe, smacked his lips together, and cracked his knuckles.

"I'm off to change," he said.

The Gundersons were quite a bit younger than I. John Gunderson produced several amazingly unfunny sitcoms, and his wife Sheryl fancied herself a writer. They had moved in behind me only a year before, and I did not know them well, mostly through bits of conversation that drifted across our pools. Once I heard John Gunderson announce to a group of friends, "We've outdone ourselves, don't you think?" And though I wasn't sure if he was referring to their party or their lives, from that point on I had harbored great ill will toward them.

I would stop my father, I decided, in whatever way necessary. I would lock him in his room if it came to that. The last thing I needed was bad publicity, the crusty old accomplice added to my list of specialties. I went outside and stood on the deck with my drink, waited for him to appear in his thief attire. It was a cool night, pleasant and quiet. I looked down at the Gundersons' house. It was almost midnight and their lights were out, although I could not tell if they were asleep or merely away for the evening. Their pool shone in the glare of security lights; rafts floated aimlessly across it.

And then I saw a black flash go by. It was so quick I nearly missed it, nearly thought it was the blink of my own eyes. A figure was kneeling at the foot of the Gundersons' eight-foot privacy fence. The figure lingered for a few moments, on hands and knees, then took something from his satchel and threw it up into the air. It was a rope ladder, it caught, and I watched my father scale it, pull the heap of himself awkwardly over the top of the fence, and disappear on the other side.

I stifled the urge to yell, watched the figure creep through the backyard from tree to tree. I stomped my foot on the deck, a sound that echoed through the neighborhood. The figure, striding ridiculously long steps toward the house, stopped and looked back, gave me the thumbs-up sign, and ducked by a bush and crawled like a foot soldier the rest of the way, to the sliding glass door that led to the Gundersons' game room.

I turned away. I had been in the Gundersons' home only once, a few weeks after they moved in, and I could not remember its layout except for the game room and living room. What could I do? I could not run after him, nor call the police. And so I waited for the sound of the alarm, trying to concoct a story for when the captured thief was linked to me, but when no sound came I looked back and the figure was gone. No alarm had sounded, no shouts, no shots.

I wished then, for just a moment, that I had gone with him, that I was on his heels as he found his way through the house, sniffing out jewelry like an animal after a bone. I imagined him passing through a darkened kitchen, heavy but sleek, knocking into a table and snagging a salt shaker in midair before it could hit the floor. I felt his breath coming fast through tight lungs as his hand, its age hidden by a thin black glove, reached into Sheryl Gunderson's jewelry box, taking the likes of things my crazy father could never give to my mother, had now to give to women who were nearly strangers.

Someone will shoot him, I thought, shaking away the movie in my head. He would bungle something, bump into a china cabinet and be shot dead by an officer from a security company who was answering the call of the silent alarm. I would have to claim him. His clothes were in my house.

I thought then of my mother, of her clothes, which my father had laundered along with his and mine for two months after her death. I had grieved for my mother only in a material, nine-year-old way, missed what she gave me and not what she was. Images of her struck me occasionally in my adult life: a tall woman leaning over a stove, her apron rumpled, her forehead shiny with sweat, stirring something in a big black pot. A woman in front of me on a bicycle, where I sat in a safety seat wearing my father's old combat helmet, watching her hair whip behind her, her shoulders thin and taut. And she and my father, on snowy days, swinging me out from our front porch into the mounds of snow below. This was not an image but a sensation: my shoulders stretching, my legs flinging loose like a puppet's, the brittle air stinging my eyes, and then the flying.

"They up?"

I dropped my drink; the coffee mug cracked in half on the

wooden deck. My father was standing beside me, the ski mask over his face.

"You're completely insane," I said.

He reached into his satchel, pulled out a fistful of earrings. "Diamonds," he said, pulling up his mask to look. His face was bright red. "Seven pairs. No more mamby-pamby. Now you wanna tell me what I can't do?"

"How'd you get in? What about the alarm?"

"A little pair of hedge clippers'll do the trick. It was a cheap one anyway, the base of the fence, easy to find." He smiled. "I coulda done it in my sleep."

I felt myself smile too. It was the bourbon, I reasoned, certainly not the fact that my father had just burgled my neighbors.

"I'm beat," he said, putting his hands on his hips. "The sides ache, you know, climbing and crawling. Going up to bed. Maybe tomorrow we'll drive around, stake out a little, you know?"

"Dad."

"Huh?"

"You know I can't let this go on."

He didn't answer. He walked into the house, pulling off his ski mask and shaking the static from his hair.

I watched him go up the stairs, and was starting for another drink when I heard something out front. I went to the entryway and parted the blinds slightly. A security guard was walking up my driveway, followed by John Gunderson. I stepped away from the window, listened for my father, then opened the door.

"Hello John," I said. It's a role, I thought. A role that is not crusty. "What can I do for you?"

John nodded, cleared his throat. The security guard stood by him, hulking and silent, his eyes hard with suspicion.

"Jack, this is very awkward," John said. "I'll just come out with it. This afternoon I saw you and an old man sitting by your pool. We've had a robbery—"

I registered perfect shock.

"—yeah, we were asleep, but Sheryl thought she heard something so we got up to take a look and . . . we've got this monitor, see, and when we saw that some jewelry was gone we ran the tape back five minutes and that man who was sitting by your pool was staring straight into the camera."

"There must be a mistake," I said. Switch roles, I thought. The fake-out would not work, not when video was involved.

"No mistake, Jack," he said. "I thought I should come to you first, though, before I made an official complaint."

I glanced at the officer.

"Private security," John said. "He's not official."

The guard's face didn't change. He was paid, I thought, to look earnest, although sometimes he must want to burst out laughing.

"I'm stumped, frankly," I said, stalling.

"May we come in, sir?" the security guard asked.

I stepped aside to let them in, and out of the corner of my eye I saw my father descending the stairs, his robe on and his hair wet, just out of the shower. It was too late to stop him.

"Who is it, Jack?" he asked, and then he winked at me, actually winked at me.

John Gunderson looked startled. "That's him," he said. "That's the man on the camera."

My father stuck his hand out. "I'm Jack's dad," he said. "Glad to meet you."

John looked from me to my father. The guard shifted, poised for trouble, as if my father at any moment might draw a pistol from his robe. And I had a crazy thought, looking at John and his security guard, that they once were swung between their parents as I was, lifted into the snow, that they laughed at the thud they made when they landed.

"Where have you been this evening, sir?" the guard said.

"I was in bed, then I got hot and took a shower," my father said. "Hot as hell out here."

"I'm sorry," John said. "But I know that's not true."

"Sure it is." My father yawned. "You stay up late in California, don't you? I'm from Maine, myself."

It was quite possibly the worst acting job I had ever seen. On top of that, his face was on tape, after all, his mask rolled up so as not to block his goddamn peripheral vision.

"Go on back to bed, Dad," I said. "Let me talk to these gentlemen." I shot John a look, gave my father a slight shove toward the stairs.

"Nice meeting you," he said to John. "Hope to see you again."

I walked John and the guard out front, then took John's arm and led him a little away from the porch.

"I'm sorry, Jack, but I know it was him," John said.

"You're right. It was him. My father has"—I racked my brain—". . . spells," I finished. "He's not well. He's dying, he's got some crazy idea he's a thief."

John frowned. "Alzheimer's?"

"Maybe. The doctors don't know for sure; it takes him over, he probably doesn't even remember doing it. Whatever it is it's humiliating."

I paused a minute to let this all sink in. John Gunderson shook his head, touched the top of his curly blond hair.

"Let me go get whatever he took. I'll send him back to the home tomorrow. I never should have let him out in the first place."

John looked unsure. He didn't know me well.

"Please," I said.

"You were in the first movie I ever saw." John smiled and poked me in the chest with a finger. "I was eight years old." This fact had sealed something for him. "Can you bring the stuff down now? Sheryl's . . . you know."

"You bet. Let's just keep it quiet, okay? No need to get the press or the cops involved, right?"

"Sure thing, Jack. Sorry all the way around. What a mess."

I found my father in his room, dressed in the clothes he had come in eight days before, his suitcase on his lap. The jewelry sat on the dresser.

"Go on, take it," he said, waving his hand in the air. "I heard you through the window."

"I'm sorry."

He shook his head. "I had 'em fooled, Jack. With that shower thing. They never could have pinned it on me."

"I've got to take this stuff."

"I know. And I'm going back to the home, right? And I've got goddamn Alzheimer's."

"I saved your ass. I lied to save you. You were on the video camera."

"I'd rather go to jail than be some crazy old man who doesn't know what he's doing. It's embarrassing, Jack."

I picked up the jewelry in my fist, went back downstairs. My father's gray windbreaker was hanging on the knob of the entry-way closet, and I took a pair of earrings, diamonds with a star sapphire in the center, and slipped them into his pocket.

I would see these earrings again, recognize them immediately on the ears of Edna Burnside, whom I introduced myself to at my father's funeral after he died suddenly of a stroke six months after his visit. All the women at the funeral were wearing jewels much fancier than the housedresses and worn wool coats they donned at the cemetery, and among the jewels were several bracelets and necklaces of Lorraine's which, at the moment I was slipping Sheryl Gunderson's earrings into his jacket, my father was up-stairs stealing from me. His final theft, clean and professional, would not be noticed for weeks, not until Lorraine was moving out of our house and discovered her most secret and luxurious stash, hidden in a drawer among slips and stockings, had completely vanished.

"Life is rocky sometimes," John Gunderson said to me when I handed him the remaining six pairs of Sheryl's earrings. "We all have hurdles, don't we Jack? Rough seas, bumpy roads . . ."

"Indeed," I said.

He pocketed the jewelry, sighed, seemed lost in this thought of his. Finally the security guard caught his attention by sneez-

ing, and the two of them left, although not before John invited
me to Sheryl's birthday party the following weekend.

"Maybe next year," I said.

Inside, my father was already standing in the hall with his
suitcase.

"I called a cab. I'll catch a plane back tonight. Back to the
home for the mentally hopeless."

"I made it up, Dad. I was acting, playing the role, remember?"

He pursed his lips. "It's a blurry line sometimes, eh Jack?"

I started to speak, to answer him, but a horn sounded, and my
father's eyebrows shot up. "A cab in five minutes." He shook his
head. "Fantasyland."

Had it been a movie, I would have gone with him. Instead, I
handed him his jacket. "Don't forget this."

He took it, slipped it on, then brushed past me and went out
the door. When he reached the cab he turned and thrust his
hands into his pockets. "See you, Jack," he called gruffly. Then,
in the glare of the streetlight, I saw the outline of his fist clench
inside his pocket, and he smiled.

COUNTING THE
WAYS

KATY'S mother was a real piece of work. She lived like
a hermit in a crappy little apartment in Newark, listening to talk
radio and working crossword puzzles and—from what I could
tell—just waiting to keel over dead. This broke Katy's heart, but
she kept trying. One Sunday a month we'd drive out to Newark
and I'd always end up balancing her mom's checkbook or un-
sticking her windows while Katy threw out all the stuff in the
cupboards and the fridge that had gone rotten since the last time
we'd been there. It wasn't even that the old lady's mind was
gone; she just didn't give a shit whether her checkbook was balanced or her windows could open or her food was any good. She
didn't give a shit about anything, as far as I could tell. She only
spoke when asked a direct question, and her answers were always
polite and indifferent and short, like she was being interviewed
for a job she didn't really want; she looked right through Katy
like a pane of glass. Personally, I thought she was crazy, but I
knew better than to say this to Katy.

Finally the old lady died, sat down at the breakfast table one
morning and stroked out. It was me who found her, three days
later. She had nose dived into the *Times* crossword with her hair
still wet from the shower, so when I turned her over her whole

face was stained black with crossword clues. I didn't tell Katy about that part. No matter how much pain a person's caused you, you don't need to hear something like that.

Her mother left us twenty-eight thousand dollars. We needed it. I had lost my job as assistant manager of the Econo Lodge North three months before when they closed the motel. To make up for it they made me a part-time desk clerk at Econo Lodge West, but between that and Katy's lousy data entry job we were bringing in just enough to cover rent and food and the lamest insurance you could get. The inheritance was enough to let us think about moving out of the city, maybe having a kid. But Katy said no. Katy wanted to blow the money. Maybe if the auction hadn't been that week, things would have turned out different. Maybe she'd have come to her senses and maybe now we'd be living in a little house in the suburbs, playing peekaboo with Joel Junior. But no. We were sitting in front of *Entertainment Tonight* the day after the funeral and on comes the story about the auction.

"I want to buy one of those dresses," Katy said, pointing at the TV with her fork. "Okay? Let's?"

"Babe," I said. "What're you gonna do with a dress like that? Where you gonna wear it? The grocery store?"

She shot me The Look. "Don't make me say that it's really *my* money," she said, setting down her fork on the coffee table. "I don't want to have to say that."

I looked at the dresses on TV. Most of them were pretty ugly. I wouldn't have paid a hundred bucks for them, much less the thirty, forty grand they were going for.

"I want to do something crazy with that money," she said. "Something totally unexpected. Can you understand that, Joel? I want to do something she never would have done in a million years."

"It's crazy," I said. "I'll give you that much."

"I've always loved the princess," she said sadly. This was news to me. She had never mentioned loving the princess before, but I could see she had her mind made up. You're probably thinking I could have talked her out of it, probably thinking I could have stood up right then and said, Listen, babe, it's me or the dress. But the truth is Katy had had a pretty shitty life. There weren't very many things in the world that made her happy, and if she thought buying one of the princess's old dresses was going to do the trick, then I was willing to give it a try. I had never seen the money, never laid a finger on one dollar of it. It was like Monopoly, like when you pass GO and then wind up on INCOME TAX; the money just stays in the little slots of the bank.

When I got home from my shift the next night the dress was in the bedroom. It was mossy green, had a curvy neck and a skirt as round as a barrel. She had bought a mannequin too, an extra hundred, and stood it up in the corner of the bedroom, by the wastebasket. The mannequin had a shiny bald head and its eyes were the size of peanuts.

"Whadya think?" Katy asked. She was standing beside the mannequin with her hand resting easy on its shoulder, like they had been best friends since kindergarten.

"It looks like an alien," I said.

She scowled. "The dress, Joel. What do you think of the dress?"

"It's nice," I said. What could I say? It was a green dress.

"She danced in this," Katy said, running her hand down the sleeve. "She went to a ball and danced in it. Her skin touched it."

I unbuttoned my yellow Econo Lodge shirt and bowed to the mannequin. "Princess," I said, holding out my hand, "may I have this dance?" I lifted the mannequin and held it tight against me, pressed my nose against its hard shoulder. The dress smelled like a sandwich bag. I twirled the mannequin around and around in circles, singing oom-pah-pah oom-pah-pah, until I was dizzy. Katy sat down on the bed, clapping and laughing.

"Look at you," she said. "My handsome prince."

I set the mannequin back in the corner, yanked Katy off the bed and danced her once around the room and then down onto the covers. "Princess," I said, not cracking a smile, "may I have this dance?"

She giggled, got all red in the face. This never stopped amazing me, how your own wife could blush when you started making love to her, get all lit up like you had just moseyed out of a fairy tale. Like she didn't throw your underwear in the washing machine every week and pick your hair out of the shower drain. Like she didn't know what a screwup you really were.

Besides Katy, I've fallen in love with lots of stuff. I've fallen in love with baseball bats and old shirts and fat steaks and movie theaters and street signs and tire swings. But that summer I fell in love with a green dress. We both did. We treated that dress like a lover and a baby and the old blind family dog. Part of it was the money, but it was more than that. It was the way she stood there in the corner, hearing everything and seeing everything, taking it all in and never asking for anything back. We stopped smoking in the bedroom. When it was nice out we'd open the blinds and let the afternoon sun fall on the green shoulders.

One day I came home from the grocery store and heard Katy talking in the bedroom. I set down my bags real quiet and snuck up to the door, took a peek in. She was trying on scarves; there were a whole bunch of them lying on the bed. She tied a blue one around her neck and posed in front of the mannequin.

"What do you think?" she asked. "Is it me?"

"It's you," I said.

She whirled around. For a second the moment sat there on the fence and I thought she was going to get pissed off at me for spying. But then she smiled.

"Let's go out for dinner," she said.

"Out?" I couldn't remember the last time we had been out to

dinner. I couldn't remember the last time we had eaten off anything besides the coffee table.

"You're off tonight, right? So let's forget the groceries and go out and have a fancy meal."

"What are we celebrating?" I asked.

"Why do we have to be celebrating anything?" she asked. She went into the bathroom to brush her hair and I stood there looking at the mannequin, wishing I could think of some way to pay her back for this rare gift. We had had her two weeks and the magic hadn't worn off yet.

"Hey Joel?"

I went into the bathroom, wrapped my arms around my wife and looked at us in the mirror.

"Knock knock," she said.

This got me. I used to do this all the time and it always drove her crazy. Every time I had said "Knock knock" in the last six months she had rolled her eyes and said "Nobody's home."

"Who's there?" I said.

"Mannequin."

"Mannequin who?"

"Mannequin use a night out with my husband."

I kissed her shoulder. "Baby," I said. "That really stinks."

A week later Katy started having troubles at the office. She said that one of the bosses was getting a little friendly with his hands, massaging her neck and stuff when she was at the computer. I didn't know whether to really believe her. She wasn't exactly a liar, but sometimes she exaggerated things a little. I offered to go down to the office and kick the guy's ass anyway.

"Be realistic," she said to me. "What good would that do?"

We were in bed. She had her head in the crook of my elbow and my arm was already asleep, my fingers tingling. We slept this way most of the time. Sometimes when I got up in the morning my arm hung dead for ten, fifteen minutes.

"Why don't you report him?" I asked.

"Yeah Joel, I'm sure they'd fire him right away."

"So quit," I said. "Get a new job."

"We're barely making it as it is," she said. She sat up and I shook her weight out of my arm. She reached into her night-stand and got out a pack of smokes.

"Babe," I said, tossing my head at the mannequin. "Come on, you don't want her to stink, do ya?"

She fingered the unlit cigarette. "We're pathetic," she said, to no one in particular. "I can't even afford to be out of work for a goddamn week."

This was pretty much true. My hours at the motel were get-ting cut back, a little at a time. I was looking around for more work, but I couldn't find anything—there are about eleven thou-sand guys in the city with desk clerk experience.

"I'll get a second job," I said. "Flip burgers or something."

The cigarette broke in her fist. "You're not going to flip burg-ers!" she screamed at me. She screamed every once in a while, out of the blue, a big fat one like this. Then she said this thing that killed me: "Just imagine what my mother would say about you flipping burgers!"

I sat bolt up in bed, spoke before I had time to think. "If you're so worried what your mother would say, then why in hell did we blow her thirty grand on a goddamn dress?"

She shot out of bed and stormed out of the room. I took a breath and started counting. This was something I'd learned from my dad. Don't go after them, he'd said about women. Just start counting and they'll be back before you hit ten. But the truth was, I'd never been able to do it, not with Katy. Usually by the time I hit three I was so full of guilt and panic that I'd go af-ter her. This time I made it to five before I hauled myself out of bed and slunk into the living room. She was sitting on the couch sucking on a cigarette.

"Babe . . ." I said.

"You love the dress!" she shouted. "I've seen you, you know, looking at her all moony-eyed. You love it just as much as I do!"

"You're right," I said, leaning against the doorway, looking at my bare feet. "Settle down, babe, you're right. I'm sorry."

But she wasn't listening. The magic of the dress had finally worn off, and she had tunneled back to that place inside her, the place with no name and no address and no closing time. There was a time once when I thought that place made her beautiful, and I wished I could go there with her. But now, I thought, that place was just like her mother's—cold and quiet and too small to hold more than one.

So then it was that Saturday night. I was behind the desk at work, checking some fat couple in, and the man looked up at me and said, "Have you heard?"

"What's that?" I said, grabbing his room key from the box on the wall. People were always trying to tell me things, having been cooped up in their cars all day. I usually listened halfway, tops.

"The princess and her boyfriend had a car accident," the wife said. "The boyfriend is dead and the princess might be too."

My shift was just about over. I didn't want to call Katy; I figured if she had heard she would have called me at the motel, and I didn't want to have to tell her over the phone. I sat there picking my fingernails until the overnight guy came in, then beat it home.

There are things you can never forget. For me, there's three. When I was eleven I saw one of the kids in my class get his foot run over by a school bus. He was joking around, sticking his foot under the tire and then pulling it out—he was one of those kids who was always doing stuff like that, anything for an audience. He must have thought the bus driver saw him the whole time, but then I heard the groan of the bus starting up and the tire rolled over this kid's foot. And the kid just stood there—what else could he do?—just stood there, his face flush against the side of the yellow bus and his Reebok flat as a dollar bill on the pavement. Then one time, about a year before I met Katy, I saw an old Chinese woman fixing her wig on the bus in the middle of the night. She was using the window as a mirror and kept tilting the wig this way and that, but no matter which way she tilted it it still looked like a hat. Then finally she just took the wig off and held it between her knees and pet it like a cat.

Anyway, the other one happened that Saturday night. I swung open the door to the apartment and I see Katy. She's sitting on the couch all wrapped up in a brown blanket, like a big caterpillar. Right next to her, standing propped up on the middle cushion of the couch, is the mannequin. They're both looking at the TV with exactly the same expression. Then the guy on TV goes, "The silence is disturbing."

"Is she dead?" I asked.

"We don't know," Katy said. She didn't even look at me, and I wondered who the "we" was. We as in the whole world, every poor slob sitting on pins and needles in front of his TV at midnight, or we as in Katy and the mannequin.

"What happened?" I asked.

"They were going home," she said. She didn't say anything else, so I went into the kitchen and grabbed a couple beers, then went and sat on the couch, on the other side of the mannequin. I cracked my beer, then Katy's, but when I held it across the mannequin's skinny shins to her she wouldn't take it.

"We've had no word for some time now," the TV guy said. "One can only imagine this means that the injuries to the princess may be more severe than we were first led to believe."

"Jesus," I said. I reached across the mannequin again, set my hand on the blanket where I supposed Katy's knee would be, but she jiggled herself and my hand fell away. The TV guy had his fingers pressed against his earpiece. Behind him, a whole bunch of people were sprinting around with sheets of paper in their fists, yelling stuff. I started to feel sick to my stomach and I wanted to turn the TV off, take my wife for a drive, pick up

vanilla shakes like we used to do and drive around the city talking about what we were going to be when we finally grew up.

"We're getting a report now," the TV guy said slowly. I'll give
him this: he didn't look excited, like some news guys look when
they tell you a plane exploded or somebody shot up a McDonald's. He looked like he'd rather be about anywhere other than
our living room. "We're getting an unconfirmed report now," he
said, "that the princess has died."

I felt my hand moving again. I was going for Katy, but I
felt the folds of the green dress under my fingers and I held tight.
I wanted to throw up, so I set down my beer. Katy whispered
something.

"What?" I said.

"It's unconfirmed," she said. "Unconfirmed."

But I knew what that meant, only that it meant nobody important would say the words, but that the words were out there
already, and I imagined how she was lying on a table in a room
all alone and the tubes were already unhooked and she was already growing cold.

Two hours after it was confirmed and Katy had baby-stepped her
caterpillar-self to bed, I was still sitting in the living room, my
feet on the coffee table, stinking drunk and chain smoking the
last of the cigarettes we had in the house. They were showing
pictures of the car being towed out of the tunnel, its front end
crunched like a wad of tinfoil. The mannequin was still standing
beside me, and I was just plastered enough to pull it over onto my
lap, let its little head rest on my thigh. I straightened out the
sleeves, set her collar right. You're probably thinking I kissed it
or something, but I didn't. It wouldn't have seemed right, even as
drunk as I was, them talking about how she had held out alive for
a time, asking questions, how it took an hour just to cut her out
of the car, how her boys were likely just now being woken by
their father. I just let my hand rest on the sleeve and stared at the

pictures which were clouded from the smoke in the room and blurry from the beer in my head.

It was around four when some old English lady being interviewed looked right out of the TV at me and said: "It's terrible to say at a time of such tragedy, but the dresses that were recently sold at auction will no doubt now be worth ten times what they were worth last month."

My cigarette dropped from my lips to my shirt. I slowly lifted my hand off the dress. My first thought was to act right then, like I could have stumbled out onto the street with the mannequin and there'd be some guy waiting on the sidewalk with a sack of money. I'd redeem the dress like a lottery ticket, have it over and done with by the time Katy woke up in the morning, deal with her tears by showing her the money—in my crazy head all three hundred grand of it in cash, a big pile of it in the middle of the room—enough to buy a house away from the city and live off of, even, not work for a long, long time. Then I thought of Katy's mom, dead like the princess, how it had turned out we had done something smart with the cash after all, invested in fate and hit the jackpot. I thought of the old lady with her face stained black and her life stained black and how it had seemed all she would leave in her wake was that damned blackness. But here life had twisted itself up again in that way it does when you least expect it, and now—on what was surely the blackest of nights for so many—me and Katy finally had a little bit of light.

"No way," Katy said, pouring herself a tumbler of grapefruit juice. "No fucking way."

I was prepared for this, had woken up early with only a baby hangover, and figured out how to convince her.

"Listen babe," I said. "Here's the first thing we do with the money. We fly over there, over to England, and we go to the funeral. We can put flowers and stuff at the gate."

"Everybody gets to put flowers at the gate," she said, swallowing a handful of aspirin with her juice. "What we have is special. It was special before and it's even more special now."

"Listen to this, though," I said. "We can send flowers every week. We can get a different bouquet every week and send it over there, for the rest of our lives if we want to."

"We bought that dress with my mother's money," she said. "That may not mean anything to you, but it means something to me."

"Babe," I said. "Your mom's dead. Don't you think it's about time to move on?"

Move on. These words were foreign to Katy; it was scrawled all over her blank face. I might as well have been trying to teach the roaches in the corner to tie my shoes.

"The dress makes me happy," she said flatly.

Okay, I may not have known what happy was, but I was pretty sure I knew what it wasn't. It wasn't crying in the shower and it wasn't staring at the same page of a magazine for an hour. It wasn't reading birthday cards your mother sent you when you were a kid and it wasn't making up stories about what people did to you at work. It wasn't crossing your arms when your husband put his hand on your breast and it sure as hell wasn't swallowing a handful of aspirin with your fucking grapefruit juice.

I should have said all this—hell, *any* of it—but all I could think of to say right then was: "We can have a real life, Katy."

She dropped her tumbler in the sink and it clattered around in there for a couple seconds. Then everything was quiet, except a couple blocks away some idiot's car alarm was going off, whooping it up for the whole neighborhood.

"We *have* a real life," Katy said.

"Okay, then. A better real life."

She snorted, and I felt it coming. There was only one thing to do when it was coming and that was to batten down the hatches, close myself up so whatever shit that was about to fly out of her mouth wouldn't be able to touch me.

"Better?" she said. "How are we going to be better? You'll still be the same old stupid you and I'll still be the same old stupid me and we'll still be the same old stupid us. What's so fucking great about that?"

She walked off and left me standing there in the kitchen. A second later the bathroom door slammed shut. At this point there was no point. She had hit bottom and I had learned a long time ago that when she was at the bottom there was no rope long enough for me to haul her out with. I could have waltzed her into heaven and she would have looked around and snorted and said, "What's so fucking great about this?"

I made it to seven before I found myself standing in front of the bathroom door. The wood was cheap, thin enough to knock down in one good shove; the sound of my knocking was the familiar hollow.

"Babe?" I said. "Hey babe . . . you okay?"

When I got home from work that night the apartment was spanking clean and there was a bottle of champagne sitting in the middle of the coffee table.

"Katy?" I yelled.

She came floating out of the bedroom, all light and smiles, pointed a long finger at me and broke into song. "If you were a rich man," she sang. "Ya-da-da-da-da-da-ya-da-da-da-da-da-da-da-doo."

Katy was in *Fiddler on the Roof* when she was in high school. Every once in a while she would dredge it up and start singing her lungs out. One time the guy next door banged on the wall with a pan until she quit.

"What's up?" I asked.

She stopped ya-da-da-da-doing. "What's up?" she said. "We are. We're up a hundred and ninety thousand bucks."

My legs went Jell-O and I sat down on the couch. "You sold it?"

"Not yet," she said. "But I found a buyer. I called the auction house and it turns out there's this guy who's come into town. He's buying a whole bunch of 'em. We're not the only ones with brains."

"A hundred and ninety grand?"

"That was his offer," she said. "I took it."

I was reeling. I wanted to ask her what it was that made her change her mind, after all that crap about her mother, all that crap about *happy*. But no, I thought. Why start? This was what I wanted anyway, wasn't it? But even then I knew that what I wanted had nothing to do with what went on in her mind. Her mind, shifting like the wind, sweeping me along whichever way she wanted to go.

"Open the champagne," she said. "There's more in the fridge. I quit my job. And I told that moron downstairs we'd be moving at the end of the month."

"Moving?"

She sat down next to me and grabbed onto my arm. "Like we always talked about," she said. "We can buy a house now. We can get a big dumb dog from the pound and roast marshmallows in the fireplace every night. Can you imagine?"

Looking at her face, her eyes, I could. She popped the cork on the champagne and it exploded all over us, knocking me out of my daze. I licked it off her neck and sucked it out of her hair and we kissed on the couch until the bottle was gone. Then we went for bottle number two and headed for the bedroom.

She was there in the corner. Katy had gotten the plastic bag out of the closet and it was hanging over the curtain rod.

"Let's put it in the bag," Katy said.

"Now?" I was already halfway out of my pants.

"Now," she said. She flopped down across the bed on her stomach and propped her chin in her palms. "We don't want to look at the dress all night," she said. "We'll feel too guilty."

I stepped out of my pants and approached the mannequin. Suddenly I felt funny, standing there in my shorts about to take her dress off. I felt like I was in seventh grade, and I blushed.

"Come on, Joel," Katy said. "Strip her."

I wondered if she was getting some kind of weird kick out of this. You never knew with Katy, what was going to get her going.

I stepped carefully behind the mannequin and started working on the top button. It was tiny, tight, and I was drunk. I couldn't get the damn thing unbuttoned. I looked over her shoulder at Katy.

"You do it," I said.

She smiled. "Uh-uh."

I was starting to get pissed off. I kept fumbling with the button and finally got it done, went on to the next one. I was wondering who else had unbuttoned this dress. The prince? Some lover? Or the maid or whatever, like in movies, some fat-cheeked woman who undressed the princess and then tucked her into bed with a cup of tea. Finally I reached the last button. I came around to the front of the mannequin and gathered the skirt in my hands, gently. I lifted it up above her hips. I had to swivel the arms up to get the thing over her head. When it was off I slipped the bag over it and went out into the living room, hung it up in the kitchen. Then I went back into the bedroom. Katy's clothes were in a pile on the floor and she was under the sheets, staring up at the ceiling.

"Want some more champagne?" I asked.

"Nope," she said. "Just you."

I clicked off the lights, stripped off the rest of my clothes and slid under the sheets beside her.

"Are you happy?" I asked her.

"Yeah," she said.

"Really?"

"Really," she said.

I had drunk enough champagne to flatten a moose, but after Katy fell asleep I lay wide-eyed in the dark bedroom. I kept trying to think about what I was going to do with all that money, but every so often a sweep of lights came across the window and lit up the mannequin and I couldn't help but stare. She was pale and naked, her breasts nippleless, the area between her legs smooth and sexless like a Lone Ranger toy I had when I was a kid who when I took off his cowboy pants had no penis, no balls, no nothing. Her arms were still swiveled above her head and there was a wide scar across her waist where tomorrow we would unscrew her and toss her into the dumpster out back.

She was looking at me with those little eyes.

We were set to meet the buyer at the Hilton. At ten-thirty we rolled out of bed, grabbed the dress, went out front and waved down a cab. I was starting to feel kind of sick, the champagne from last night still churning in my stomach. I glanced over at Katy; she looked a little sad and I wanted to ask her what she was thinking, but she was watching the city go by and didn't look in the mood for talking. By the time we were in the lobby of the Hilton I could taste bile at the back of my throat and I told Katy to go on up to the guy's room, that I had to go in the john and toss the cookies, but that I didn't want the guy to think we were standing him up. She looked mad.

"Baby," I said. "I don't want to barf all over the guy."

"Okay," she said. "But hurry up."

It took me about ten minutes to get presentable after puking. I washed up and slicked down my hair and tucked in my shirt and then took the elevator up to the sixth floor, where the buyer was staying. I went to room 604 and gave the door a good rap. The guy opened it. He was an old guy, had a gray beard and rectangle glasses. He was wearing a red cardigan sweater that was kind of faded and he didn't look like a guy who'd have a million bucks to spend on dresses. Or anything, for that matter.

He put out his hand. "Joel?"

"Yessir," I said, like he was the principal of the Hilton.

"You're late," he said.

I shrugged. "Had to make a pit stop." I wished I'd have thought of something else to say, but it got out before I could think of anything better. I looked over his shoulder for Katy.

"Where's the dress?" he asked.

Right then, I could hear all the clocks in the hotel ticking. I could hear them so clear it was like they were right behind my eyes, ticking away my life.

"My wife has it," I said. "Isn't she here?"

He stepped back to show me the room. There was a glass pitcher of Bloody Mary on the desk and three gray suits hanging in the closet and half a muffin on the table and Granny Clampett was on the TV playing the ukulele.

"She came up before me," I said. "She must have got off at the wrong floor or something."

"Shall we have a drink while we wait?"

"Sure," I said. I followed him into the room. My palms were all sweaty, but I took the glass from his hand, drank the Bloody Mary in one big gulp. He raised his eyebrows and poured me another, then flipped off the TV. I sat down on the bed, holding the glass in my hands. My eyes were shaking.

"How long have you had the piece?"

I looked up at him. I must have looked like a retard. I felt like a retard, my thoughts slogging through my head like syrup.

"The dress," he said. "How long have you had it?"

" 'Bout a month."

He looked at his watch. "Should we call the front desk?"

"Why?"

"To see if your wife's there . . . lost perhaps."

I shook my head slowly. "She's not lost," I said. "She's gone."

He sat down beside me and the weight of the bed shifted and I nearly fell over on top of him. In a way I wished I had. Sometimes you just want to feel somebody's hands on you.

"Gone?"

"She must have changed her mind," I said. I set the Bloody Mary on the floor between my feet. I wondered when the idea had hit her, wondered if it was when she was standing in the elevator all by herself with the dress, waiting for the doors to slide open. Or maybe it was before then, in the cab when she was staring out the window, the excitement worn off and the realization coming on that it was just another sad day like all the rest.

"Surely she just—" the guy started.

"No," I said. "No, I should have figured."

He frowned. I thought he was going to be mad about the dress, tell me to get the hell out of his room. He had other fish to fry. He was a big shot. But then he stood up and looked into the mirror, stared into it and looked past himself for a long time.

"Well," he said finally, "she must be waiting for you somewhere."

"Yeah," I said. "She must be." Then I started counting, without even thinking about it. On three I looked at my feet, waited for them to move, but they didn't. On six I took a deep breath and waited for myself to stand up, but I didn't. I couldn't figure it out. When I hit ten I got up slow, but instead of heading for the door I walked to the window, looked down six floors to the sidewalk in front of the hotel.

She was there, all right. The dress was folded over her arm and her hair was taking the breeze. She was just waiting, standing still in the middle of the crowds moving past. She must have been thinking I would be down any second to tell her I didn't care that she had changed her mind, to tell her that whatever she wanted was a-okay with me. And who could blame her? What had I ever done to make her think I could do anything else?

I opened my mouth to ask the guy if he minded if I hung around a little while longer, maybe have another drink with him. But when I turned my head to ask he was already behind me holding out my glass. I took it from him and turned back to the window, looked below me at all the people swarming the sidewalks who didn't know me and didn't know Katy and didn't know that this time she was going to wait there forever. The old guy in the sweater, he was the only one who knew. And I didn't even know his name.

THE GREATER
GRACE OF CARLISLE

m Y mother, beside herself with loss, spent thirty-five thousand dollars on lottery tickets in nine months. It was Mr. Jenkins from next door, the official neighborhood bearer of bad news, who finally called to tell me.

"You know I don't like to tattle . . ." he began. He ended with: "We thought you should know."

I thanked him. I had thanked him as a teenager when he peeled my cat off the road and brought her limp body to our front door. Funny, the things you wind up thanking people for.

My stepfather Walt had died the previous January, after almost two years of battling stomach cancer. Through it all, my mother was the poster child for well-adjusted spouses of the terminally ill. For twenty-one months, her good will and sound judgment bordered on the psychotic. And after he died—after he finally, finally died—she seemed fine. Well, not exactly fine, but up to speed for a grieving widow. She wept as she packed away his flannel shirts, even had a session of grief therapy with the minister at their Methodist church. And then she seemed to go on with her life. I stayed with her for two weeks and then returned to my own crumbling world, a thousand miles away. As I bitched my way through a separation and second divorce in Arizona, my mother was going crazy in Illinois, trying desperately to win the lottery.

"We've discussed it," Mr. Jenkins said. I didn't ask who the "we" was, probably him and his tropical fish. "We think you should probably come for a visit."

At the time, I was doing temp work in Phoenix. I was also doing temp life. I had moved there only a year before with my ex-husband; what friends I had made were the wives and girlfriends of the men at his office, women I had not had time to bond with profoundly enough to warrant the inevitable awkwardness of postdivorce friendship. I had suffered through this period before, with another husband in another state, so I knew what to expect: the occasional pity call, an offer for a lunch date that never materialized, empty well-wishing that was worse than no wishing at all.

"I'll be there," I told Mr. Jenkins.

And so I returned to my childhood home of Carlisle, Illinois, population thirty-five hundred morons. My mother didn't admit anything for two days. I was afraid to spring it on her, wary of pointing fingers at my mother, who (like the good fourth-grade teacher she had been for thirty-two years) always told me that when you point a finger at somebody you've got three fingers pointing back at yourself. I didn't want any more fingers pointed at me for the rest of my life, so I tried the subtle approach.

Day one:

"Where's your car?"

"I didn't need it any longer. I sold it."

"Don't you ever drive anywhere?"

"I can walk to the market, you know. I'm not feeble."

•

Night one:
   "You still have that stock?"
   "The market is shaky. Besides, that was Walt's game."

Day two:
   "Where's Grandma's silver?"
   "I don't know. Somewhere in the attic."
   "I sure love that silver."
   "Really? I always thought it was ugly."

Night two:
   "You still have that teacher's pension coming, don't you?"
   She put down her glass of wine. "Chatty Chatty Kathy," she said, raising her eyebrows. "I'm beginning to think you have an ulterior motive."
   "I just want to make sure you're financially sound," I said. "Don't you read magazines? All these eighty-five-year-olds end up working the drive-thru window at McDonald's because they've squandered their money."
   "I won't be working at McDonald's," she said.
   "I was just—"
   "It's sad," she said. "I thought we were fairly close. I'd expect this type of sneaky behavior from your brothers, but not you. Next thing you'll be following me to the market."
   "Why would I want to follow you to the market?"
   She smiled slyly. "What time is it?"
   I looked at my watch.
   "Don't tell me," she said. She closed her eyes and held up her left hand as if testing the breeze in the dining room. "It's six forty-five, isn't it?"
   I was impressed. "How'd you know?"
   "I've developed a sixth sense. You know what happens in twelve minutes?"

"What?"

She rose from her chair. "We get rich."

She dropped her napkin on the table and drifted off into the living room. A moment later I joined her. She was sitting cross-legged on the floor in front of the television, a six-inch stack of lottery tickets in front of her.

"How many?" I asked.

"Hm?" she said. "Three hundred."

I sunk down on the couch. "You spend three hundred dollars a day on lottery tickets?"

"Don't be stupid. They only draw three times a week."

"Nine hundred dollars a week."

"Nine hundred dollars will be like nine cents in about five minutes."

I sat back and crossed my legs. Following a brief trumpet fan-fare, the lottery man came on the TV, wearing a suit and tie and a hairpiece of questionable quality. A scantily clad Illinois farm girl with hair down to her butt was pulling ping-pong balls out of a chute. The numbers were announced. My mother scribbled them down on a sheet of paper, then began going through her tickets.

"Gimme half," I said. "I'll help."

"Not a chance," she said.

So I sat there and watched her go through her tickets. It took twenty minutes. She scanned each one and set it off to her right, beside her on the floor. She didn't speak, made no noises of de-feat. When she had scanned the last ticket (twice, I noticed) she picked up the pile and stood up and left me sitting there on the couch. I followed her into the kitchen. She threw the tickets away and started washing the dishes.

"Well?" I said.

"Well what?"

"You didn't win."

She turned off the water, turned to me. "No," she said. "I just didn't win *today*. On Wednesday I'll have three hundred more chances."

"I don't think this is very healthy," I said.

"Neither is smoking," she said.

"I don't smoke."

"I didn't say that you did. But millions of people do. And millions of people drive their cars too fast and millions of people clog their veins with cholesterol and none of those people are healthy either."

"Mother . . ." I said.

"Don't you 'Mother' me."

"How much money do you have left?"

"Enough."

I laughed. "Enough for what?"

She turned back to the dishes. "Enough to buy you a plane ticket back to Phoenix."

The next morning when I went out for the mail, Mr. Jenkins was next door mowing his lawn on his riding mower. His lawn was no larger than your average suburban lawn, but he had owned this riding mower for as long as I could remember and mowed his lawn at least twice a week. While I stood at the mailbox he waved me over and cut the engine. He wiped sweat from his brow, although it was cool out, September, and I wondered how somebody could get sweaty riding around on a little tractor.

"How's Hildy?" he asked. "You get her to stop buying those tickets?"

"Not yet," I said.

He took my arm. "You know whatcha do?" he said. "Across town, there's this church. They got anonymous groups there for everything, got people all over this area coming in to get fixed. They got your standard Triple A, then they got anonymous shoppers, anonymous dopers, anonymous homosexuals, anonymous spouses." He leaned into me. "They even got that anonymous necrophiliacs."

"Nymphomaniacs?" I ventured.

"The sex junkies," he said. "Whatever you call them. And they got one for gamblers, like Hildy. You should take her down there, Kathy, see if they can set her straight."

"I'm not sure that's necessary," I said.

He shrugged. "She's your family." He reached to start the mower, but then stopped. "Heard you got divorced again," he said. He landed on the "again" like he had run over a dog with his lawnmower.

"Yes," I said.

"You're a good girl, Kathy," he said. "Why don't the boys see that?"

"I don't know, Mr. Jenkins," I said.

In junior high school my best friend Melinda Marietta used to say, "You can't get your period in Carlisle without half the town knowing about it." Pretty close to the truth. Out for my daily walk that afternoon, I felt the eyes of the people on our block settle on me from porches and bay windows, and I imagined they all knew that my mother was spending her teacher's pension (more importantly, *their* tax dollars after all) on lottery tickets. I ignored them as best I could, walked down the ragged sidewalks, past the old post office, and found myself on Locust Street. Before I knew it—yes, idiot Mr. Jenkins had gotten to me—I was standing in front of a fading brick building, one of two hundred just like it in the historic district, with a white sign on the front that said THE GREATER GRACE OF CARLISLE. It didn't really look like a church, although the glass doors were propped open and I could hear what sounded like a choir singing from the basement. I took a few steps in and looked around. There was an office, and the door was open, so I peeked in and saw a heavy man in jeans and a turtleneck sweater sitting at a desk reading a magazine.

"Hello?" I said.

He looked up from his magazine, smiled. "What can I do for you?"

"I heard you have groups here," I said. "I was looking for something for a friend, something about gambling?"

He motioned me to a chair. I sat down and he folded his hands on the desk in front of him. "First," he said. "Let me tell you. We are all gamblers, and we are all anonymous. There's no need to be ashamed."

"It's not me," I said. "It's my mother."

"Ah-hah?" he said, intrigued. "Your mother . . . I see. What's her addiction?"

"She buys lottery tickets."

He slammed his fist down on the desk. "Goddamn lottery," he shouted. "Goddamn helps-the-schools-helps-the-elderly-helps-the-highways lottery."

"This a common problem?"

He breathed a heavy sigh. "Problem, no. Epidemic, yes," he said. "Does your mother know you're here?"

"God no," I said. "She doesn't think she has a problem. Or an epidemic."

"They never do," he said wistfully. He stared off over my head for a moment, frowning at the concept of addiction as if it were hovering in the doorway. "You'll have to get her to come to group," he finally said. "We meet every Wednesday, in the basement." He smiled at the voices rising from the floor. "That's our choir."

"It's not singers anonymous?"

He didn't smile. "Wednesday," he said. "Tomorrow night, seven o'clock. It's an intimate group. You may come if you wish, the first time, if necessary."

"You mean if I have to drag her?"

"We don't drag," he said sincerely. "We nudge."

"Who runs the group?"

"I do," he said. He extended his hand across the desk. "I'm Brother James."

I didn't ask whose brother he was. I had enough brothers, four of them, all in their forties and far away with wives and kids whose names I usually couldn't remember. To them, all of them, Carlisle, Illinois, was like a disease; it had infected my mother and they were damned if it was going to get them too. I understood how they felt. The most famous people from our town were Eddie Wills, who got a football scholarship to the University of Illinois, sat on the Fighting Illini bench for four years, and returned to open a shoe store downtown, and Bud Porter, who stepped on a land mine in Vietnam and for twenty-five years had sat every day at the table at the Sheetz drinking cherry Slurpees and letting kids touch his fiberglass leg. The sign when you entered Carlisle read, HOME OF THE 3A CROSS COUNTRY DISTRICT CHAMPS, 1984—GO BEES!

My mother was in her vegetable garden. It's small, but prosperous, supplying most of the neighborhood with tomatoes and green peppers for the majority of the summer. She was wearing jeans and a White Sox sweatshirt, some ragged gardening gloves with faded strawberries, and a big splintering straw hat. This was the kind of image that humiliated me as a child. Now, standing at the kitchen window, I found it comforting.

"Turn on the hose!" she shouted at me.

I went out back and turned the rusty knob, then joined her beside her tomato plants, which were withering, already preparing themselves for the first frost, their timely deaths.

"Long walk," she said.

I sat down on the soft earth beside her, twisted some grass around my finger.

"Did you go down to the park?" she asked. "Those ducks are—"

"You've got a problem," I said.

She adjusted her hat. "Just one?"

"Haha."

"All right, what's my problem?"

"You're going to be broke in a year. You're going to lose this house, Mother."

"Not if I win."

"You're not going to win," I said. "You are never going to win."

She set down her spade, brushed some hair from her forehead with the back of her hand. "What makes you so sure?"

"I'm just sure."

"That's a lousy answer. I wouldn't accept that from fourth graders, so I'm certainly not going to accept it from you."

"Okay, then," I said. "What makes you so sure you will win?"

"God told me."

This gave me pause. Then I thought: This is my mother; things can only get so weird. "Tell me you're kidding," I said.

"Of course I'm kidding. What kind of lunatic do you think I am?"

"Listen," I said. "There's this church down on Locust, this—"

"I know all about it," she interrupted. "Mr. Jenkins keeps leaving their literature in my mailbox. I see him sneaking out there after he thinks I've gone to bed."

"Go for me," I said. "Just one time, just tomorrow night. Go for me."

"I can't tomorrow. There's a drawing."

"So you can tape it and watch it when we get home," I said. "Look at it this way—you can live in blissful denial for an extra two hours."

She smiled wistfully, and a gust of wind knocked her hat to the ground.

When Brother James said the group was intimate, he wasn't kidding. There were only three people there when we arrived, besides the Brother. My mother took one look at them sitting around the little conference table in the basement and turned back toward the stairs. I blocked her exit and she entered the room with a flourish, as if she were entering a cocktail party.

"Hello all," she said cheerily.

"Come in, come in," Brother James said, waving us to join.

The members of the group introduced themselves. Rick, definitely a corn farmer, was there with his tense wife. It was his first time too. Then there was a tall and lanky guy, Andy. He was unshaven and wore a ripped army jacket, looked like he had made a wrong turn on the way to the homeless shelter.

Farmer Rick, it turned out, had a card problem. He had played a friendly game of poker with some friends once a week for twenty years, so friendly, in fact, that he had lost all of his wife's savings to his friends.

"And Andy?" Brother James said.

"I'm your run-of-the-mill equestrian addict," Andy said.

"Forgive me," the farmer's wife said, her cheeks reddening. "We're new at this. Is that like LSD?"

Brother James sighed. "Andy bets money on horses," he said. "And Hildegard?"

"Hildy, please," my mother said, flushing.

"Hildy?"

"I enjoy buying a few lottery tickets," she said.

I snorted, and she shot me a look.

"What's a few?" Brother James asked.

I opened my mouth but he raised a hand to shush me.

"Three hundred each drawing," my mother said. "But I have plenty of money, I can afford it. And I'm not addicted."

"See?" Farmer Rick said to his wife. "See? What'd I tell you?"

My mother, sensing an ally, turned to him and smiled. "You're not addicted either?"

"Oh, that's not what I meant," he said. "No, I was just telling her earlier that it could be worse, that I could be buying lottery tickets."

My mother paused. Then she said, "This from a poker player."

"Well now," Brother James said, grasping his hands together. "Looks like it's time for our first lesson. We work as a team. A team. We're here to support each other, not cut each other down."

"But it's much more interesting that way, Brother James," Andy piped in.

Brother James grimaced. "Andy's been with us for quite a while," he said. "He's seen a lot of people cured, haven't you Andy?"

Andy shrugged. "Sure. Then most of them start turning up on Mondays."

"What's Mondays?" the farmer's wife asked hopefully.

"AA," Andy said.

Brother James forced a chuckle. Andy smiled. He had incredibly straight teeth. He caught me looking at him and winked in my direction. My mother sighed.

After the group was over, Andy cornered me outside the door. "I'm heading over to the track," he said. "You want to come?"

"No thanks," I said. "What track?"

"Kathy . . ." my mother said. "We need to get home."

"Fairmount Park," Andy said. He stretched his long arms over his head, yawned.

"That's three hours from here," I said.

"My lucky track this month," he said. "Wanna come? Great nachos."

"I hate nachos," I said.

He shrugged. "Suit yourself, daughter of lottery addict."

"I'm not an addict," my mother said.

This time, I refused to watch the drawing with her. I sat on my old bed in my old room flipping through an old *People* magazine. Princess Diana was on the cover, smiling with baby William, having no idea she would end up bulimic and divorced and dead.

My mother appeared in the doorway, holding a single ticket in the air.

"What?" I asked. I had an instant—a tiny and surprisingly beautiful moment—where I believed that she had actually won.

"Four numbers," she said. "*Four* numbers. I'm getting closer, Kathy."

I threw the magazine on my lap. "You're not getting closer. Luck is not something you can get *closer* at. Did I dream it, or were you not once a teacher, a fairly sensible person?"

"How can you sit with those people for two hours and come away thinking I have a problem? They're obviously far worse off than I am."

"Mother, addiction is not measured by degrees."

"Oh my God," she said. "You're becoming one of them. You left your life in Phoenix for this?"

Then, sitting there in my old bed in my old room with my old mother, I felt myself start to crack. It crept in my toes and up my thighs and through my stomach and past my heart and into my head and—much to my humiliation—I felt my eyes well up with tears. It wasn't that I had left anything behind in Phoenix that got to me; it was that I *hadn't* left anything behind in Phoenix. You should not be thirty-five years old and be able to leave your home behind with a day's notice. There should be people to call, troubles to iron out, explanations to give. But there had been none of that. I didn't even get a newspaper.

"Oh, honey," my mother said, coming to my bed. "I didn't mean it. You're nothing like them, really."

"I can't believe I'm back in this town," I said. "I can't believe I'm back in this shitty town and it's exactly the same as when I left and *I'm* exactly the same as when I left."

"No you're not," she said, petting my cheek. "You're all grown up."

I swatted her hand away. "What exactly has changed? I'm a two-time loser, Mother. Just ask Mr. Jenkins or anybody else in the neighborhood."

"I'm a two-time loser too," she said.

"Yeah, but one of your husbands died, so it doesn't really count. You're like a two-time loser with an asterisk. You didn't *blow it* twice."

"Maybe I did," she said. "How do you know? Maybe I was blowing it with Walt and he died before we could go through with the divorce."

I wiped my nose, amazed. "Is that true?"

"Well no," she said. "But it could be. All I'm saying is there are always circumstances, honey. It's never as simple as it sounds. Who cares what people think?"

"You don't care that people think you're crazy?"

"I care that my daughter thinks I'm crazy. That's why I went tonight. But no, it makes no difference to me what other people think."

"Then you're crazy," I said.

"Maybe so," she said. She stood up, waved the nearly successful lottery ticket above my bed. "But when I'm rich everyone will say I'm merely eccentric."

The next day I was lying on the couch watching TV when my mother stuck her head into the living room. "I don't mean to alarm you," she said. "But your boyfriend's been sitting in the front yard for ten minutes."

"Funny," I said, not raising my head from the pillow.

"I'm not kidding." She opened the blinds, and I sat up to see out the window. Andy, the pony better, was sitting beside the mailbox. When he saw us looking at him he waved.

"What's he doing here?"

"I couldn't imagine."

"Maybe he's here for you, you know, for a little impromptu group therapy."

"I sincerely doubt that," she said. "Now go on out and tell him to stop lazing in the front yard before Mr. Jenkins calls the police."

I got up and went warily to the door, opened it and stepped out onto the porch.

"Hi there," he called. "Want to go for a stroll?"

"A what?"

"You know," he said, standing. "A stroll. Like walking, but happier."

Well, I decided, I hadn't had my walk today. And I did need to get him off the yard. I closed the front door and joined him in the lawn and he started walking.

"What're you up to today?" he asked.

"Nothing," I said. "TV."

"Sounds fun," he said. I couldn't tell if he was being sarcastic or not, so I didn't respond.

"You're from around here, aren't you?" Andy asked.

"How'd you guess? The tattoo on my forehead?"

"I remember you," he said. "You were a couple years ahead of me in high school. When'd you graduate? Eighty-two? Eighty-three?"

"Something like that," I said.

"You played the cello, right?"

"I supported the cello," I said. "And I moved the bow. I wouldn't go so far as to say I played it."

He grinned. We turned the corner onto Spruce Street, heading toward the Sheetz. "Check this out," he said. He reached into his pocket and pulled out a wad of bills. "Ninety bucks," he said. "Down to five measly dollars and I nailed the last race. There's some grace for you, huh? Can I buy you a Slurpee?"

We were now standing in front of the Sheetz. School had let out, and there were several little Bees buzzing around, smoking cigarettes and flirting. We went into the store. Bud Porter was sitting with his leg propped up in the booth, slurping his Slurpee and reading *Mad* magazine.

"Hey Budster," Andy said.

"Hey Andster," Bud Porter said.

I let Andy buy me a grape Slurpee and we went and sat down in the booth behind Bud Porter.

"Blowing off work for a date, Andy?" Bud asked, not looking up from his magazine.

"I got the afternoon off," Andy said.

"You have a job?" I asked. Too late I tried to keep the astonishment out of my voice.

"Sure," he said. "Whatdya think, I rob banks to support my habit?"

"I knew a guy who robbed banks," Bud Porter said behind me.

I ignored him. "What do you do?" I asked Andy.

"Fix up furniture," he said. "I work with about a dozen second-hand shops in the area, fix up crappy stuff until it looks like something somebody'd want in their house. Makes me enough money to support the old addiction."

"You don't seem to have any problem with the old addiction."

"Why should I?" he asked. "If you're going to be addicted to something, you may as well be addicted to something that there's some possible payoff for in the end. Sure, I could smoke dope. But what good would that do me? Least this way I have a chance."

"A chance for what?"

"Winning," he said. "Like your mom. She could be drinking, you know. Or stuffing herself with doughnuts. You should be glad she's only buying lottery tickets. Gambling is the optimist's addiction. It's the only one that makes any sense."

"So why do you go to group if you don't care if you're addicted?"

"You know what I love about this town?" he asked, skirting my question. "There's always the same number of people. I've been here my whole life and as many people as die or move out get born or move in. That always amazes me. Lots of little towns die, lots of towns boom. Not many towns are consistently thirty-five hundred people."

"You *like* that?"

"Good for my business," he said. "Somebody's always getting rid of furniture but somebody's always looking to buy it. And all the stuff along the street on junk pickup, you wonder where it's coming from. Attics. All the attics in this town are full. But they

keep being full. I don't exactly understand it; I just ride with it."
He took a drink from his Slurpee. "Whada you do? You don't still
live here, do you?"

"God no," I said. "I live in Phoenix. I'll be going back soon."

"I knew a guy from Phoenix," Bud said from behind me. He
lowered his magazine when I turned around. "He ate dirt."

"Wanna get some air?" Andy asked.

I was already standing. Andy said good-bye to Bud and we
went back out onto the street.

"Old Bud," Andy said, heading back down Spruce. "He's got
some stories. What's your story?"

"I don't have a story," I said. "Well, I do, but it's dull."

"I doubt that."

"Why?"

He shrugged. "Dunno," he said. "You just seem like someone
with a story. You've got that aura about you."

"Give me a break," I said. "Your horses have auras?"

"Sure do," he said. "I'm just not so great at reading them most
of the time."

We walked home. How many times had I walked this walk?
Grade school, high school, girls beside me, boys beside me, no
one beside me. It made me sick to think about; I could have
closed my eyes and not missed a step.

"So what's in Phoenix?" Andy asked suddenly.

"My ex-husband's job," I said.

"I can see why you're so anxious to get back," he said. If I'd
known him better, I probably would have hit him.

"Thanks for letting me buy you a Slurpee," he said.

"You're welcome."

"Maybe I'll see you around?"

"Maybe," I said. But I didn't really think so.

My mother was acting weird. Well, weirder. I'd walk into a room
and catch her staring out the window. At the dinner table I'd offer her a cup of coffee three times before she'd even hear me.

One morning she was in the shower for over an hour, and twice in the middle of the night I heard her above me, rummaging around in the attic. I wondered if she were up there looking for things she could sell.

The third time, I got out of bed and went up the attic stairs to find her. She was sitting on an old dining room chair with a needlepoint pillow for a seat cushion. She had a box on her lap and was sifting through it.

"Whatcha looking at?" I asked.

She looked up, didn't seem surprised that I was standing there.

"Just things," she said. "Old Christmas cards, things like that."

"How come?"

She shrugged. "You're here," she said. "It's too sad for an old woman living alone to get up in the middle of the night to look through things in her attic. Makes it better if there's someone else in the house." She held up a construction paper Santa Claus. "Dear Mommy and Daddy," she read off the back. "Hohoho and I want some Hot Wheels. Love Teddy." She smiled. "He has a Camaro now."

"See, he got his Hot Wheels," I said. I rested my hand on an old TV. "Was this Daddy's?" I asked. "One of the things he was going to fix up?"

"Your father . . ." she said. My whole life, this had been my mother's response to any mention of her first husband. "Your father . . ." and nothing more. What else needed to be said?

"You gonna go to that group tomorrow?" I asked.

"I might," she said. "You have a message you want me to relay?"

"No," I said.

"He seems like a nice enough boy. Isn't often someone sits quietly in your front yard and waits to be acknowledged."

I was sleepy, and this pissed me off. "What are you saying, Mother? You think I should go on dates to the track with him? Make this gambling thing a real family affair?"

She was quiet. She set the box down at her feet. Then she said, "Honey, don't you ever just want to hope for something?"

"I think I've hoped enough, thanks," I said.

She gazed at the backs of her hands. "You know what Walt used to say about you? He used to say you were the best of the bunch. That girl, he said, is going places."

"And here I am," I said. "In the attic in the middle of the night with my depressed mother, rooting through boxes of Christmas cards and petting broken-down TVs. Old Walt was a smart guy. I've really gone places, haven't I?"

"When are you leaving?" she asked wearily.

The question took me aback. "I don't know."

"Well figure it out," she said. "I was wrong about having some-one else in the house. It's actually sadder when the other person is you, Kathy. Why don't you just pack your bags and go back to Phoenix? Better yet, why don't you get even farther away? Would that make you happy?"

"Good night," I said.

"Will you be leaving tomorrow?"

"I can't leave tomorrow," I said. "Tomorrow you might win the lottery."

But she didn't. While she was at group I watched the drawing without her, went through all her tickets and then left the pile sitting on the floor, wrote "Too Bad" on the top ticket and went upstairs to my room. I lay in the dark and thought about what I would do when I got back to Phoenix. I pictured myself walking into my apartment and opening my mail, checking my answering machine. I saw myself changing into sweatpants and sitting down on the couch and flipping on the television, listening to the Mallorys next door fighting about whose turn it was to take the dog out.

I heard my mother come into the house. I thought she would come to my room, say good night, at least make some snide com-ment about the note I had left for her on her stack of loser tick-ets. But after the stairs creaked I heard her go into her room,

then the sounds of the faucet, the flush of the toilet, the soft din
of the TV in her bedroom. Fine, I thought. And I closed my eyes.

In the middle of the night I was awakened by a noise. I sat up
in bed and heard it again, hail pelting against my window. But it
was only mid-September, no time for hail, even in stupid Illinois.
I got up and went to the window, opened the blinds. Andy was
standing on our front lawn, a handful of pebbles in his hand. He
waved.

I closed the blinds, stood there motionless for a moment.
Then I slipped on a loose sweatshirt and went downstairs,
opened the front door. He was sitting in the middle of the lawn,
juggling the pebbles.

"What's up?" he said.

"What time is it?" I asked.

"I dunno," he said. "Three-something."

I shivered against the cold and he stood up.

"Just back from your lucky track?" I asked.

He shrugged. "Not so lucky anymore."

"Didn't win the last race?"

"I didn't even make it to the last race."

A light came on in Mr. Jenkins's upstairs. I saw the blinds split,
and I took a step back into the darkened doorway. Andy smiled.

"You gonna get busted? Think he might call your mom?"

"Police is more like it."

He shrugged. "No warrants on me," he said. "You want to
walk?"

"Is the Sheetz open?"

"Open all night," he said. "But I'm busted. Wanna go down to
the park?"

I looked up at Mr. Jenkins's window, could see his shadow
against the blinds. He was probably worried Andy was going to
mess with his lawn.

"Okay," I said. "Let's go."

The park was four blocks away, where our street dead-ended. I
had played there with my brothers as a child, spent years wading

in the pond looking for gold until my oldest brother finally broke the news that I wouldn't find any.

"Saw your mom at group tonight," Andy said. "She's gonna be okay, you know? I think she'll stop pretty soon with the tickets. Sometimes people have weird ways of grieving."

"I guess," I said, unconvinced.

"She cracks me up, though. Spent half the meeting correcting the Brother's grammar."

"Why do you keep going?" I asked.

He shoved his hands in his pockets, shrugged. "I don't know," he said. "Goodwill, I guess. I take it wherever I can get it, and there's not much at the track."

"I'm going back to Phoenix," I said. "Tomorrow probably."

He stopped. We were at the entrance of the park. On the banks of the small pond, dozens of ducks slept in groups of two and threes.

"How come?" he asked.

"My mother's had it with me."

"That's too bad," he said.

"Yeah?"

He started walking again. "I used to run in this park all the time," he said.

"Whatdya mean run?"

"You know, run. Like walking, but faster. I did cross country in high school. I loved this place. Some of the guys always wanted to run on the track, around and around and around a thousand times. I always thought it was a lot nicer here."

"You were a Bee?"

He grinned. "I was more than a Bee. I was a District Champ Bee, 1984."

"No way," I said. "The sign. On the sign, that's you?"

"Me and five other guys, yeah."

I shook my head. "You're famous."

"Yep," he said. "That's me. Famous Andy of Carlisle. Ran the course in 19:41 thirteen years ago. Unforgettable, huh?"

"You still run?"

"Once in a while," he said. "At night, sometimes, when I go out the turnstile at the track, I just start sprinting to my car. Never much of a sprinter, but it feels good sometimes, to just turn on the gas."

He squatted down on the ground beside the pond. There were two ducks about twenty feet to our left, sound asleep beside each other, their beaks buried in their wings.

"Look at those guys," Andy said. "They're probably thankful there's no one pelting bread at them."

"I can't believe they're just sitting there," I said. "They usually get scared."

"They'll wake up in a minute," he said. "Pick up our scent or something, open their eyes and waddle away."

"How do you know?"

"I told you. I love this place."

I squatted down beside him.

"Hey, wanna wager?" he asked.

"On what?"

"I'll take the one on the right, the one with the brown in his feathers. He wakes up first, you buy me a Slurpee. The other one wakes up, you owe me nothing."

"Is that it?"

"What do you mean, is that it? A wager's a simple thing, Kathy."

"Okay," I said. "You're on."

I extended my hand and he took it. I tensed up for a second, almost lost my balance in my squat, and he gripped my fingers to keep me from falling.

"No cheating," he whispered. "You gotta stay still, or the bet's off."

So we sat there in silence, still holding hands, listening to the distant hum of the highway. There was no moon, and the water in the pond looked black and deep, reflectionless. My duck, the one on the left, fluttered a wing at a passing moth, seemed just on the verge of opening his eyes. I felt Andy's breath catch, and I thought of what my mother had said, about wanting to hope for something. A cool breeze from the west slid through the park; the leaves above us rustled and Andy's duck twitched his feathers in his sleep.

"Wake up," I whispered. "Wake up."

EXPLAINING DEATH
TO THE DOG

a F T E R the baby died, I found it imperative that my German shepherd Stu understand and accept the concept of death. The first week wasn't so bad, what with all our friends and relatives around, smothering Stu with affection. And Todd was home from work that week, dumping well-meaning casseroles accidentally-on-purpose onto the kitchen floor for Stu to indulge in. So Stu didn't notice the absence so much, didn't seem to. He trotted around the house happily, oblivious to the fact that the baby, who he had had a big hand in raising, was missing.

Then the party ended. Guests cried the last of their tears at my front door, said "What a waste" for the thousandth and final time, and made their separate ways back to their separate lives, lives that sailed along quite smoothly despite the absence of the infant whom they had been mourning for a good seven or eight days.

Todd went back to work; packed up his briefcase and kissed me good-bye. He nearly tripped over Stu in his rush to get out of the house. He wanted away, wanted to get busy again. Stu and I stood at the window and watched him drive away. Stu looked up at me and then back at the empty driveway. He lay down on the floor in front of the window. I sat next to him and rubbed his stomach. He sighed.

What to do with the baby dead? No diapers, no screaming, no feeding. What had I done before the baby? I had been pregnant. Pregnant for longer than she had been alive. And what had I done before I got pregnant? I tried to remember. I supposed I had cleaned the house. Cooked. Taken Stu to the park. It didn't seem like it could have been nearly enough to take up a whole day.

In the afternoon I made myself a sandwich from one of the two whole hams that were still in the refrigerator and sat in front of the television. I waited for Stu, waited for him to emerge from wherever he was sleeping, jingling and jangling his way to a possible meal. The house was quiet. Still, very still. The morning the baby died Todd shook me awake to the stillness and said, "Listen, she's sleeping . . ."

I set my sandwich on the coffee table and got up to look for Stu. I called him a few times. Nothing. I walked through the house, from room to room. I found him upstairs, in the baby's room. The room was empty, except for one chair. Todd and the relatives had cleaned it out the day of the funeral because they said it was just too sad to look at. They stashed the crib in the back of a stranger's car and carted it away, hid the dolls and mobiles with the cobwebs in the basement. Then Todd's mother said the room looked so bare, so she had taken a chair from our bedroom and set it by the window. It looked unnatural by itself in the baby's room. Worse than bare. Just awkward.

Stu was lying in the middle of the empty room. His ears were back and his eyes open. He didn't raise his head when I came in. He just followed me with his eyes.

"Stu," I said. "Stu, what the hell are you doing?"

He looked like he had eaten too much casserole, was what it was, looked like he might toss his canine cookies at any moment. He stood up lazily. He walked in circles around the room. You could tell he was looking for the baby.

"No," I said. I called him to me and patted his head. "No more baby," I said. "Baby's gone."

He looked at me with the universal blank dog look. He had

no idea what I was talking about. "No baby," I said again. It was then that I realized the impossibility of the situation. It wasn't even like trying to explain death to a child. The dog simply couldn't understand the language. He had a brain the size of a walnut and all he knew was that the baby wasn't where she was supposed to be. I imagined it must be even worse than knowing the baby was dead. At least Todd had been able to logically spell it out for me that morning to get me to stop shaking her and trying to wake her up, hold the little girl up in my face, point to the chest. NO BREATHING.

It was then I decided that I needed to teach Stu about death, whatever the cost. I figured he had a right to know, being a member of the family.

"Come on, boy," I said. He slunk out of the baby's room behind me. I closed the door.

On the coffee table we had a book. A big *Life* magazine book. *Best of Life*, something like that. I gave Stu part of my ham sandwich to lure him up on the couch with me. I opened the book out on the coffee table, paged through it, looking for the sixties, the best lesson of death on film.

"Lookee," I said. I turned the dog's head toward the contorted face of Lee Harvey Oswald, and the man behind him, a man whose name they never mentioned, looking like he might jump right out of his skin from the shock of it. Oswald was holding his stomach, hadn't even hit the floor. "Dead," I said. "Stu, it's dead."

Stu didn't seem to see the picture. He looked at the book, sure, but there was nothing in his eyes that said that he saw the proverbial farm being bought. The way he looked at it, it could have been a picture of a rolling wheat field. I turned the page, looking for something bigger, and found a two-page spread from Memphis, 1968, the man dead on the balcony, people pointing out into the sky. It was big; you couldn't miss it.

"Death," I said to Stu. "No more."

Again Stu glanced at the picture, then back at my ham sand-

wich. I jabbed my finger on Martin Luther King, Jr., held the picture up in Stu's face, and still his eyes didn't focus on it. What
was I expecting? I don't know. If Todd had been there he would
have clapped the book shut and told me the dog didn't know
what the hell was going on and he'd be over it in a day and a half
anyway. But Todd was gone. Strange things happen when you're
alone in the house with pets all day.

In the middle of the night I woke up and heard the baby crying. I sat up and reached for my glasses before I remembered. It
was not a staggering thing. It washed over me slowly, the way you
remember what day it is when you wake up in the morning. I
looked at Todd lying on his stomach next to me, the side of his
face pressed to the pillow, his mouth open. The first week it was
him who couldn't sleep. I'd open my eyes and he'd be sitting up
in bed, his back against the wall, staring into space. The minister
had come by and Todd told him about not being able to sleep.
The minister said it was probably guilt, thinking that if he'd been
awake when the baby started dying he could have done something about it. After that I guess Todd became comfortable with
the guilt, because he didn't sit up nights anymore.

"Todd?" I said.

In the corner, Stu raised his head and looked at me.

"Todd?" I said again. I didn't have the courage to touch him,
to wake him up and force him to share the grief, to try to explain
to me why I might have heard the baby crying when the baby
had been dead for over a week. I lay back down next to him and
started thinking about the simplicity of a dog's mind. I tried to
think of a way to explain to Stu just exactly what was going on.

The morning was cool and dark. It was May and the natural
order of things said it should have been warm and bright. But the
natural order of things was wrong, so it was ugly out. Todd sat at
breakfast and looked at the newspaper in much the same way Stu
had looked at the coffee table book. His spoon went from the ce-
real bowl to his mouth without being led by anything but habit.
I stared at him and he didn't even notice.

"I think Stu misses the baby," I said.

He looked up from the paper, his mouth open and his eyes empty like he was a vegetable. "What?"

"Yesterday he was lying in her room."

"Close the door," Todd said.

"I was thinking," I said. "I was trying to figure out how to get it across to him that she's not coming back."

Todd put his spoon down. "Why would you think something like that?" he asked.

"I just thought it was interesting. I wondered how dogs understand those kinds of things."

"What are you doing today?" Todd asked. "Why don't you call somebody for lunch?"

"No one wants to have lunch with me," I said.

Todd sighed, looked at me like I was the baby squirming around while he was trying to get the diaper on. "We'll go out tonight, then," he said, but he wasn't even looking at me. He was looking over my shoulder out the back door, out into the grayness that was passing itself off as morning.

The house was clean. Relatives had occupied their time and their minds by picking up the place before the funeral gathering, and Todd and I hadn't done enough to mess anything up since then. And there was no cooking to do. I decided I would go ahead and take Stu to the park, force him down the slide for a good laugh, spin us both around on the merry-go-round just for a change of pace. There would be no baby carriage to drag through the sand, no need to worry about it slipping from my grip and careening down a hill into the creek. The park was different with no baby. It seemed much safer.

Then we found the squirrel. Stu walked right past it, didn't even notice, but I saw it. It was lying on its side in the grass. Its mouth was open, its eyes empty holes. Other than that it was fine. Perfectly whole, not the work of a cat or a child with a BB gun.

"Stu," I said. "Stu, come here baby." He stopped, turned back, then trotted to where I was kneeling on the ground. He saw the squirrel and stopped for a second. He looked at me. I reached out to touch the squirrel and Stu took a step back. Its fur was damp and brittle. Stu walked up to the squirrel, then turned his head away and looked at me like I had gotten him into something he wasn't near ready for. A fly landed on the squirrel's head and crawled into the empty eye socket.

"Stu," I said. "This is important." I took hold of his head and turned it toward the rodent. I pushed his nose a little closer to the body. "The squirrel's dead," I said. "You understand?"

Squirrels, I could hear Stu thinking. I chase these things. This squirrel is not running.

Stu backed away from the animal. I tried to hold on to him but he pulled me backward and I fell from my knees onto the wet grass. Stu ran in circles around me, afraid he was in trouble.

So we were going to go out for dinner. Todd came home and sat on the couch in a heap. His tie was askew and his hair mussed. I asked him if he had a bad day and he said he was just a little tired.

"Does that mean we're not going to dinner?" I asked.

"Dinner?" Todd leaned forward and banged the side of his head with his hand, like he was trying to get water out of his ear. "I feel like I'm all clogged up," he said.

"So we're not going out?"

He stopped banging, looked up at me. "I didn't say that," he said. "I didn't say we weren't going out." He paused. "Where do you want to go?"

"We could go someplace fancy," I said. "We haven't been someplace fancy in a long time."

For the first time he noticed the dog, lying on his side on the couch, his eyes staring absently at the ceiling.

"What's up with him?" Todd asked.

"I told you," I said. "He's confused."

"He's confused," Todd said. "The dog is confused."

"Yeah," I said. I was trying to think of a way to make a case for how confused Stu really was, but Todd didn't seem receptive to the idea.

Todd stood up and loosened his tie. "Let me change," he said. "We'll go out. I just have to get out of these clothes."

I sat on the couch with Stu and waited. Stu put his head on my thigh and looked up at me. I wanted to do something for him, take him out to dinner with us to get his mind off the mystery of the missing baby. We sat there for a few minutes. I couldn't hear any noises coming from the bedroom, so I got up and went down the hallway. I looked in the door and saw Todd sitting on the edge of the bed. He was banging the side of his head again, but this time he was crying while he was doing it. Actually he wasn't really crying. He was more making little howling noises with his throat. And he just kept whacking himself on the head.

I went back into the living room. I had a desire to get Stu off the couch and give him a push toward the bedroom, so he could stumble upon Todd and see what the death thing was all about, but I didn't have the heart.

I woke again in the middle of the night, but I didn't hear any crying. I got out of bed anyway and went into the baby's room. Stu hopped up and followed me, hopefully, but the room was still empty except for the chair by the window. Still, the dog wandered around, sniffing out the emptiness, the way he had the day before, and the day before that, and the way I realized he probably would for quite a while. I sat down in the chair by the window. Everything was quiet, and I thought of saying to Stu that that was it, that was death, the quiet. But Stu was still sniffing around the room, trying to pick up the scent of the baby, and I realized he would never understand death. All he would come to understand was that the baby was not coming back.

RECONSTRUCTION

T H E last thing Martin remembered clearly were the footsteps, and he remembered these only because they triggered in him, on a dreary cold night, an almost immediate sense of relief. They were the sounds, twenty years old now, of his three sons thundering down the driveway to greet him as he arrived home from work, the thwack of sneakers against pavement, the stampede, the promise of excitement. Martin had smiled, thinking of his children sprinting to welcome him.

Then he was tackled, crashed square in the face with something (a bottle?), kicked in the stomach, turned over and dumped out of his coat facedown onto the cold sidewalk.

"So this is what it's like," he thought. He thought it with great clarity, although he would not remember it later, would deny to himself that he thought anything, that he was conscious at all. But he was conscious. "So this is what it's like," he was thinking. And he wondered, briefly, if they would kill him, if his next sensation would be something cool pressed against the back of his head, or a shock of pain in the middle of his back, a blade with no fingerprints, or so many kicks in the head. And finally he thought of Gail—although this too he would deny to himself—and was disappointed to discover that even while facing possible death and certain injury his thoughts were as shallow and ma-nipulative as any bitter and desperate man *not* facing possible death and certain injury. "She will come to the funeral . . ." he thought, as a boot connected with his rib cage. "She will sit with the children. . . ." Laughter, above him. Someone—was this pos-sible?—said something about a frog. It was late, the street de-serted. They would get away. The police would never find them. "She'll be sorry . . ." he thought. Because it was Christmas eve, and he had had nothing better to do than to see a movie he had already seen before, then take the long way home.

Later, another clamor of voices. He squinted against harsh light; he was no longer on the street. More footsteps, but these were lighter and they squeaked instead of thwacked.

"Sir?" A nurse leaned over him, her face inches from his. She had clear braces, and he noticed how, as she spoke, the rubber bands in the back of her mouth stretched taut. "Can you tell me your name?"

He could have. He knew his name, and he said it to himself over and over in his mind, but his thoughts were jumbled and he couldn't get the words out of his mouth. After a few moments he stopped trying. In his stupor he decided that he rather liked being momentarily anonymous. It seemed pathetic and romantic to be unknown even for a short while, fitting somehow—since so little that was once his life remained—to not give himself a name.

"Sir . . . do you *know* your name?" the nurse asked again. This time, he shook his head.

He awoke Christmas morning to find a tall, frowning doctor standing over him. Three of his ribs were cracked, and his nose was broken. His cheeks ached and his ears tingled. He lifted his arm and read the plastic band that circled his wrist. John Doe, it read.

"You've had quite of time of it," the doctor said. "How're you feeling?"

"Foggy," Martin said.

The doctor nodded solemnly. "The police would like to speak with you."

Martin shook his head. "I can't tell them anything," he said. "My mind . . ." He touched his temple, then spread his fingers out in an attempt to indicate that all that had once resided therein now resided elsewhere.

"Just the same," the doctor said. "We'll give it a go."

The policemen were young, looked better suited for hall monitoring than an assault investigation. Martin imagined they would rather be home with their parents, sitting around a dying tree, ripping open packages.

"Did you see their faces?" the shorter one asked. He scratched at a pimple on his chin. Martin would not have been surprised, after Gail had kicked him out, to find himself feeling older. But instead, he found everyone else in the world—his students, his colleagues, strangers on the street—to be looking younger.

He shook his head. "I only heard them," he said. "They were laughing. I think they may have said something about a frog."

"What's that?"

Martin gingerly touched his nose, which felt something like a rotted squash. "A frog," he repeated. "Or maybe it was a dog. I'm not sure. The footsteps, really, that's all I can recall with any certainty."

"I see," the short policeman said. He scribbled something in his notebook. "You never saw them? White? Black? Young? Old?"

"I guess I was on my stomach the whole time."

The policemen frowned in unison, as if he were purposely keeping something from them, as if he and the men who had beaten him were all in this together in an attempt to frustrate the Chicago police department—and on Christmas, no less.

The short policeman flipped his notebook shut. "Dr. McMurray tells us you have amnesia," he said.

"I guess so," Martin said.

The policemen exchanged looks. "We'll do what we can."

In the afternoon he was visited by a psychiatrist, a woman with long legs and black stockings who sat so close to his bed he could feel her sweet breath on his swollen eyes.

"Don't force it," the woman said. "Let it come to you. Clear your mind and imagine a memory. Anything . . ."

She chewed on her bottom lip, turned the pen over and over in her hand.

Imagine a memory. Martin appreciated the phrasing of this. Certainly, he could imagine any number of memories, create them out of nothingness, pretend they were his own. He could imagine that he and Gail had danced to Glenn Miller tunes in their living room every night before going to bed. He could imagine that his sons had never had a day of worry or sorrow in their lives. He could imagine that he had retired from teaching at forty and spent his days building rocking chairs in his basement and listening to Cubs games which—he could imagine—they always won.

"Nothing," he said. "I'm sorry."

"Don't apologize." She leaned forward. "Quickly now—what's the last thing you remember?"

"Footsteps," he said.

"Whose?"

"Of the men," he said. "Of the men who did this to me."

"It's Christmas," she said, intensely. "Does that mean anything to you?"

"I—" he started.

"Anything at all?"

She seemed overly excited, he thought, apparently thrilled at the prospect of working with an amnesiac. This was probably the best Christmas present she could have received.

He shook his head.

She leaned back, sighed, resigned for the moment. "We're going to take your picture, John Doe," she said. "We're going to put it on the news. Someone will recognize you. That's a beginning."

"My face . . ." he said. He touched his swollen cheeks.

"The people we love always know who we are," she said. She nodded, utterly sure of this fact and proud that she had been able to enunciate it with such clarity. "They'll know you, and when you see them, it might all come back. The world you wake up in tomorrow might be your own."

And so Martin allowed them to take his picture; he could see no way around it. But he turned his face to the side, wrinkled his brow and squinted his eyes. The children would know, though. They would be worried about him. He was supposed to meet them, after all, supposed to see them today. He had presents for his grandson in the back of his car. They would find the car on the street in front of his apartment, know that he had meant to be on his way soon. But perhaps they would think he had just disappeared. Perhaps, even if they saw the paper, they would not connect the man with the butchered face to the man who was supposed to be at their table for Christmas dinner. Perhaps they would think their father had just escaped, slipped out of his own life, unable to handle the thought of Christmas without a united family, his wife opening romantic gifts from another man. In any case, the paper would not be out until morning. He had all of Christmas to be anonymous.

In the late afternoon a young man was wheeled into the room and deposited in the bed beside Martin. He was all smiles, although his arm was in a cast. He was a football player from Northwestern, had broken his arm in the Christmas Day bowl game.

"Hey there," he said, when they were left alone. "I'm Dan."

"I don't know who I am," Martin said. "I have amnesia."

"Wow." Dan's hair was red and mussed, his nose slightly off kilter from too many hits. He was sturdy, but not big—fullback, Martin guessed. "I only got a concussion," Dan said. "And this." He nodded toward his arm, then leaned over to get a better look. "What happened to you?"

"I got beat up."

Dan smiled. "Me too," he said. "And I didn't even have the ball—a helluva fake. You a football fan?"

Martin had watched perhaps a thousand football games in his forty-nine years, had held Bears season tickets since he got tenure. "I don't know," he said.

"You really can't remember *anything?*"

He shook his head. "Footsteps," he said. He was starting to like the idea of this more and more. What if all you knew, all you remembered in life, were footsteps? Always someone coming, always someone going. But no faces attached. No faces of men who would beat you and take your coat, no faces of wives and children, no faces of colleagues who met you at a bar to watch ESPN and flirt with the waitresses. He was almost certain that if he kept telling himself this that it would be true, that maybe, if he fooled everyone else long enough, he could fool himself as well. A blank slate.

The team came later. They had won, and they filled the room, eight or ten of them, Dan's closest friends. They had brought a carton of eggnog and they shared it with Martin. He held a plastic cup on his chest and drank from a long straw. He began to think of the team—these huge boys with light in their eyes—as his friends. Yes, they were the only people he knew.

"What're you gonna do now?" Dan asked him, when the team had left.

"I don't know," Martin said. "I'll guess a family might come soon. Maybe I'll remember them."

"What if you don't? My girlfriend watches this soap where a guy who had amnesia had to relearn his whole life, start from scratch, look at flash cards and stuff. That could be you, man."

Martin nodded, felt his swollen lips curl into a smile. "That could be me," he whispered.

She was there the next morning. As he had suspected, his oldest son had worried when he had not arrived for Christmas dinner, when his car had been found, packed with presents. Eventually they had called the police, then this morning seen the picture in the paper. He was no longer John Doe. He was Martin Baker again.

The psychiatrist came in, followed by Gail. "Martin, this is your wife," she said gently, the perfect setup. Gail looked pained. Ex-wife, he could see perched on her lips. Ex-wife, was what she wanted to say. But he saw her look at him, saw her cringe at the bandages wrapped around his midsection and the bruises purpling his face, and she said nothing, did not correct the psychiatrist, did not mention the new man who she had left him for. No, he could see her thinking. That little tidbit would have to wait.

"My wife," he echoed. "Yes, I—"

"He doesn't remember anything," Dan said from the bed beside him, from the other side of the curtain. "He got beat up."

Gail came and sat on the edge of the bed, touched the bandages on his stomach. "Where were you?" she asked.

Martin started to answer, started to say that he was on his way home from a movie, had decided to walk instead of catch a cab because he had nowhere to go, really, no reason to get home quickly, no dinner waiting. But he bit his tongue, shook his head. "I don't know," he said. "They told me I was found on Olive, near the Wig Shop."

Her eyes were puffy, her short black hair uncombed. She had cried, perhaps cried all night, perhaps pushed the other man away, unwilling to receive his comfort.

His oldest came nervously into the room. "Hi Dad," he said, with a slight wave. "It's Jerry."

"How long have we been married?" Martin asked Gail.

She looked at Jerry, then at the psychiatrist, then back at him. "Almost thirty years," she said.

"I don't remember anything," he said. He took her narrow hand, squeezed it, managed a small smile. "This feels familiar, though."

"It's like a soap opera," Dan said from behind the curtain.

"The doctor said it's not uncommon," Martin said. "The shock . . ."

"Yes," Gail said, squeezing back. "I'm sure you'll remember. I'm certain."

He tried to figure it out, looking at her then, feeling her cold fingers against his palm, tried to figure out at what point it had gone wrong, at what exact moment it became irrevocable, irreconcilable. It was as if he had closed his eyes, for a moment only, closed his eyes and stumbled through one day, and on the other side of that day it was too late. On what day had he closed his eyes?

His injuries, the doctors said, were not critical. He would recover fully. What he needed was stability. Later in the day he feigned sleep, strained his ears to hear Gail, Jerry, and the psychiatrist talking in the hallway.

". . . if it's permanent?" Gail's voice was low, even, controlled. He recalled being in his den one afternoon in the late summer and hearing her speak on the phone in this same voice. He shook this thought away, tried to focus on the conversation outside the door.

"Chances are . . . come back . . ." the psychiatrist said. ". . . time."

A murmur from Gail; she was practiced now, he decided, in the low tones. But then the psychiatrist's voice, distinct and full of authority: "He must feel like he has a home."

". . . not even married anymore . . ." Gail said.

"You're gonna kill him, Mom!" Jerry shouted. He was immediately hushed by the two women, but even with his voice lowered Martin could hear him clearly. "Why don't you let him back in the house? Just for a little while? Wouldn't that work?"

"Possibly," the psychiatrist said. "In cases like these, it's often just a few weeks before the memory completely returns. It will be painful, of course, but if we shock him with something right now, in this state, he might never get his memory back."

Never. He imagined the word hanging in the hallway over Gail's head, dripping with years and years of misery for everyone. He knew she would give in.

"A few weeks," the psychiatrist said again.

"Don't you owe him that?" his son asked.

And so he went home the following week, returned to the house where they had lived for so many years, where, just nine weeks before, he had packed some boxes at her request and returned his house key like a tenant. She made up a bed for him on the hide-away in the living room, conveniently, he thought, so they wouldn't have to sleep like man and wife. While he pretended to nap he heard her on the phone with the other man.

". . . only temporary . . ." she said, and he smiled, drifted off to sleep.

Later, Jerry and his wife and the grandson came, and Martin checked himself to not say the things he had always said to the baby, to not play the same games and sing the same songs. Jerry sat on the recliner drinking a beer and smiling at his little boy squealing on Martin's lap. Jerry's wife was less relaxed, kept shooting Gail profound, sad glances. The women always stick to-gether, Martin thought, and he winked at his grandson.

After they were gone, he and Gail sat on the couch and went through old photo albums. He thought of his classes at the com-munity college, students in the dark watching filmstrips, history clicking by—the Civil War in forty minutes, Reconstruction neatly swept up in the last fifteen. How many times, he won-dered, was a man given such an opportunity? Surely it had to be fate that was making them retrace their steps.

"This was in Mexico," she said. She scooted the album over onto his lap and he stared at it as blankly as possible, all the time thinking of how ill he had been. Not the water, no, but some freak flu that had forced him inside, and he and Gail and the children had sat on the big bed and played Monopoly as they could have any time at home, and yet it seemed like a vacation because they never did play Monopoly at home.

"When?" he asked.

"Fifteen years now," she said.

"We look so happy."

"You were sick," she said. "It must have been the water. Like the old joke goes."

"What old joke?"

She smiled slightly, turned the page. The youngest's birthday, hats and Styrofoam plates strewn about. Gail had dressed up as a fortune-teller, wrapped a sheet around her head and mystified the boys and girls by knowing what sports they played and what their favorite subjects were.

"I feel at home here," he said, touching the couch, nearly touching the folds of her blue skirt. "I don't actually remember it, but I have the sensation of home."

She looked down at his hand beside her thigh, and he felt outrageously cruel for a moment, for only a moment, and then remembered what she had said to him in late October. "I have no explanation," she had said. "I didn't intend for this to happen."

But it had happened, so there had to be an explanation. Such things—falling in love with other people, for instance—did not just happen with no explanation. And so he did not feel too cruel, pretending not to know her, because on that October night and from then on he had not known her, really; she had become a mystery to him, a woman who could fall in love with someone else, something that had seemed utterly beyond the realm of possibility, for either of them.

"I want to go to the zoo," he said the next morning. "Will you take me to the zoo?"

She eyed him over her coffee cup. "The zoo?"

"Where they keep the animals," he said. "On the news last night they said there was a new baby leopard. Why don't we go see the baby leopard?"

He knew she would not be able to resist. Gail had always loved the zoo, loved leaning over railings and making faces and noises at wild animals. She had taken the boys there so often when they were young that the children began to complain. "Do we have to go to the zoo?" they would say to him. "Can't we stay home?" He had rarely joined them in their weekend outings, always had a stack of exams, an overgrown lawn, a desire for quiet. Now, it seemed like the perfect way to tunnel back into her heart.

"You don't like the zoo," she said. "Besides, the doctor said you should take it easy for a while."

"We can walk slowly," he said. "And ride the train—" He caught himself. "The train was on the news last night. We can sit on the train and look from there."

She sighed. "All right," she said. "But only for a little while."

An hour later she dropped him off at the front gate and went to park the car. He sat on a stone bench, gingerly touching his aching ribs, and watched schoolchildren bundled up in coats and holding hands get off buses and scramble through the turnstiles. His broken nose throbbed from the cold, but he could not remember a time he had been so happy.

They boarded the train outside the primate house. The day was chilly but sunny, and the plastic seats on the train were warm. They wound through the llamas and elk, then made their way into Cats America, ten acres of woods and fields where, just on the other side of high fences from the train tracks, big cats lay licking themselves and staring lazily into the sky. He shifted so he would be closer to Gail, and the train slowed to a stop, the conductor announcing that in the distance to their left, under a tree, was the baby leopard and his mother. Despite their teacher's warnings, the children stood up on the train, peered off into the distance and began to squeal. Gail leaned over him and gazed at the baby leopard, and he gently squeezed her elbow.

"He's cute, isn't he?" he said.

"You think so?"

"Grrrrr," he said, and she giggled. She was wearing a big green parka that had once been Jerry's, and her cheeks were flushed red from the cold. He wanted to take her gloved hands and press them to his own cheeks, smell the leather.

The train trip ended, predictably, at the gift shop, and Martin insisted they buy matching leopard sweatshirts. Then they went into the cafeteria and sat down with hamburgers and French fries. Gail looked at her watch.

"You've been out a long time," she said.

"I feel fine," he said. He wondered if she had somewhere to be, a rendezvous with her new man, who at this very moment was waiting by the phone and cursing Martin. The thought made him smile.

"What is it?" she asked.

"It's just nice being here with you," he said. "In the cold, with all these children around."

"You really don't remember anything," she said. "Do you?"

What was there to remember? he wanted to ask. Why remember separate beds and silent dinners? Why remember the children driving cars away to colleges in the distance, leaving them there with photo albums and a marriage already infected with resignation? Why not begin again?

"Sometimes I think I remember meeting you," he said. "Last night as I was falling asleep I had an image of you standing on a street corner looking at a bus ticket and me sitting on a bus looking out the window at you."

"It was the other way around," she said. "You were looking at the ticket; I was in the window."

"Really?"

"It's good that you remember that," she said. "The doctor said your life might come to you in pieces."

Yes, he could fake it. He would begin to remember things, just bits and pieces as she said, with little well-placed errors along the way: happy instead of sad, excited instead of agitated. He would remember up to a certain point, to that day—but what was that day?—and then he would remember no more. She would have to call the man, in a month or two, tell him there was no hope, that how could she break it to this new and loving and permanently memoryless man that she had left him? How could she do this, now that she had fallen in love with him all over again?

She reached across the table and dipped a French fry into his ketchup, and he looked up and caught her eye. She smiled at him and he had a sudden urge to abandon the plan, to tell her everything. Was it guilt or pride that swelled in his chest? He was fairly certain it was pride. "Look, darling, look what I have done for you!" he would shout. "Look at the lengths I have gone to to win you back!" Her eyes would brim over with tears. "All this?" she would say, unbelieving, "All this for me? For us?"

Below the table, he dug his fingernails into his palms, deliberately inhaled the words back into his lungs. Not yet, he told himself. Not now, not yet.

The psychiatrist was suspicious. Or was it just his imagination? She folded her long black legs under her in her chair and fixed a look on him.

"The police have turned up nothing?"

"No," he said. He held on to a pink pillow with split seams, imagined the psychiatrist's patients twisting it with anger until the threads ripped loose.

"It must have been quite a shock, being struck from behind like that."

"I don't remember it, I told you."

"Yes," she said. "You told me." She fixed the look again; this time it was definitely not his imagination. A psychiatrist's sixth sense, he supposed, a liar's vibe he was sending out into the pink office.

"Do you have any memories of your marriage, Martin?"

"Just vague ones," he said. "Vague but happy."

"Happy," she said, as if the word were foreign to her, as if it had never been uttered in the office before.

"Does that surprise you?" he asked.

"No," she said. "Only that it seems unrealistic, perhaps a denial."

"How can you deny something when you don't know what something is?"

"Martin," she said solemnly, "we do it every day."

•

Dan, the football player, stopped by the house for a visit in mid-January. His arm was still in a cast, and Martin found a thick Magic Marker in the kitchen to sign it with. There was hardly any space left, but near the wrist he found a dash of white on which he wrote, "Martin/John Doe."

"I like your place," Dan said. He raised his good arm and knocked on the side of his head. "How's the noggin?"

"Little better every day," Martin said.

"I heard you're a history prof. Think you can give me a hand? I'm a week into American history and it's killing me already."

"I don't remember much history," Martin said. "I might as well be a math professor."

"I hate school," Dan said.

"I know how you feel," Martin said.

"Yeah?"

"I can imagine," Martin said.

"What I really want to do is coach," Dan said. "Go back to my old high school in Skokie, work with the backs, maybe make head coach someday."

"Sounds like a plan," Martin said.

"To me it does. But my father thinks everything related to football is a big waste of time. I mean, it's okay by him since he didn't have to pay a cent for my whole college education, but now he wants me to be a professional man, like himself, go on to grad school. He thinks I should have already gotten football out of my blood. You should see him throw, like my girlfriend. And he thinks the Bears suck."

"The Bears do suck," Martin said.

Dan laughed. "What do you know about the Bears? You wouldn't know your own name if somebody hadn't told it to you."

"Don't be so sure about that," Martin said. It got out before he could think it back, but once it was out there he was relieved. Why shouldn't he tell Dan? Dan had nothing to do with the situation, didn't know Gail, didn't know anything. Besides, he thought Dan would be impressed, and it seemed it had been a long time since he had impressed anyone.

"What?" Dan asked. "You gettin' your memory back?"

Martin leaned back in his chair and crossed his legs. "Can't get it back if it's never been gone," he said.

Dan lowered his Big Gulp from his mouth, stared at Martin. "You don't have amnesia?"

"Nope."

Dan's mouth was still hanging open; instead of impressed, he looked positively bewildered. "You're *faking*? How come?"

Martin shook his head vehemently. "No, no, no," he said. "It's not faking. I look at it as starting over."

Dan grinned wickedly, condescendingly. "Starting over? That's a stretch."

Martin shifted in his chair and then stood up, leveled a finger at Dan as if he were his densest student. "You don't know this yet," he said. He heard his voice waver, and he took a breath. "You're too young to know this, but someday you'll understand: love can make you do extraordinary things."

Dan looked puzzled. He picked up his soda and stood. "No offense, man," he said. "But what's so extraordinary about being an asshole?"

The Chicago police had suspects in his beating, a gang of teenage boys who tried to mug a plainclothes policeman and were apprehended when the posse sprinted in from an unmarked vehicle nearby. Despite Martin's insistence that he would not be able to identify them, he agreed to go down to the station and look at a lineup.

"Might surprise yourself," the sergeant said, walking Martin down the long, dingy hallway of police headquarters. "Happens all the time. Think you didn't see them but then you get a look at a face and bam, there's your guy."

Martin stepped into the identifying room, looked through the glass at five young white men slumped along a black line in the room in front of him. He let his eyes settle for a moment on each of them. There was one, the tall one on the far left, who looked vaguely familiar, something in the shape of the eyes. He felt his heart quicken. Was it possible he had actually glimpsed one of them that night, just for an instant? Was it even slightly conceivable that he had convinced himself of his own ignorance in order to avoid the repercussions of remembering?

"Well?" the sergeant asked.

No, Martin told himself. No, he had most definitely not seen them; not the one on the end, or any of the rest of them. The tall boy probably just looked like one of his students, one of a thousand faces he had passed on campus. He was playing a game with himself, the pit of guilt rising in his stomach. He thought of the look on Dan's face when he admitted to his memory. This was the payback for that.

"Sorry," he said.

"Wanna see any of 'em closer?"

"I'm not lying," he said, too loudly.

"Whoa," the sergeant said. "Didn't say you were lying, Mr. Baker."

"I know," Martin stammered. "It's just . . . frustrating."

"Relax. Take your time," the sergeant said. "Give 'em a good look now."

But he didn't want to. The teenagers depressed him, all there in a row, looking as if they should be standing outside a principal's office and not in a police lineup. Some of them were on their way to jail, no doubt, their lives spun out of control at such an early age, their histories so bleak he couldn't imagine them, and didn't want to.

"I'm sorry," he said again.

He'd sit on the stool at the kitchen counter for hours every afternoon, watching her slice vegetables, knead dough, whisk sauces.

She loved to cook, always had, loved to create as she went, with no cookbook, present her dishes—lamb and onion, pork with saffron—at the dining room table with a sweaty flourish. She did this often when the boys were young, but as they grew older, and she went back to work, it became less and less frequent. By the time the boys had moved out, she and Martin ate spaghetti almost every night, a box of noodles and a jar of sauce. In his absence, and now that he had returned, she apparently had returned to cooking with a fervor. He'd sit on his stool and listen to her murmur to the food under her breath, take in the smells of lamb and green pepper and honey and basil, watch her stir with a big plastic spoon and notice how her shoulders moved as she chopped and rolled and stirred.

"What're you looking at?" she asked one day, turning to him.

"You," he said.

"I know *that*," she said. "But what about me?"

"I just can't believe how lucky I am. Probably most people with amnesia find out they live on skid row, or nobody loves them. I feel like I hit the jackpot."

She turned back to her stirring. She was making salsa. "Martin . . ." she said, and he could feel it coming, could feel that he had pushed too far. Of course, she was getting antsy. Four weeks had passed.

"I mean I'm sure we've had our problems," he said. "I mean, who doesn't, right? But here we are, in this beautiful house, three great kids, a thirty-year marriage. We've held up pretty well, haven't we?"

"We're not perfect," she said into her salsa.

"I'm sure I'm not," he said. "But you seem pretty damn perfect." He slid off his stool and went to the counter, circled his arms around her and took the spoon from her hands, stirred the salsa slowly. She rested her hands on the counter and her chin sunk to her chest. He could feel them breathing together, the simple intake and outtake of air in tandem.

"Listen," he said. "Here's the deal. I apologize."

"For what?" she whispered.

"For whatever I may have done. For every lousy thing I ever said to you, for every time I didn't listen. For every time I might have been an asshole, and there were probably many, I'm sorry."

"Just like that," she said. "A clean slate." She turned to him, and he let go of the spoon, wrapped his arms around her waist.

"Must be nice, Martin," she said, brushing a strand of hair from her forehead. "A lump apology. Must be easy."

"It's not easy," he said. "It's not easy starting over."

But he was gleeful. It *was* easy, she was easy, everything was easy. He knew the day now, understood that there was no day, really, that he had just let their love slip away from him, slide past under his feet like ice. It was his fault, not hers, and he really could make it up to her, begin again. There was no water under the bridge, no spilled milk. He breathed in the smells of onion, pepper, tomato, breathed with her until she said she had to get back to her dinner, and chased him out of the kitchen.

They had married in February of their junior year of college, unwilling to wait until graduation as their parents encouraged, eager to cement their vows on Valentine's Day. Well, it was Gail really who had had that idea, and Martin who—still dazed by the fortune of winning her—resigned himself to taking part in all the tiresome clichés that were a requirement at a Valentine's wedding. Now, as their thirtieth anniversary approached, Martin suggested they have a party, an all-out celebration with a live band, champagne, red and white streamers, a big cake in the shape of a heart. He purposely suggested it in front of Jerry and his wife when they were over for dinner, so that Gail would not be able to weasel out of it. He saw looks go around the table. Jerry's wife's poker face had not improved, and she gazed at Gail with interest and pity.

"All right," Gail said, setting down her fork. "He wants a party, we'll give him a party."

Their other two sons returned home for the weekend of the celebration, slept in their old rooms, ate their childhood cereals, fit back into the easy rhythm of the house as if they had been gone days and not years. Over fifty people came to the party on Saturday night—longtime friends, neighbors, colleagues, even a few students. Martin promised himself he wouldn't drink, wouldn't get carried away with the occasion, tried to prepare himself for a grand performance. He knew there would be many opportunities for him to slip up and reveal himself, but he was certain that it was worth the risk: this night, surely, would be the final trump card to win back Gail permanently.

Throughout the evening several of his colleagues came up and introduced themselves awkwardly, uttering their names with excruciating care as if he were half-deaf or very old. He found himself taking glasses of champagne from them, feeling tipsy, assuring them that his mind was coming back more and more each day, that he would be back in the classroom by the following fall. One of his worst students introduced herself as one of his best students, and he let it pass with only a grin, patted her on the shoulder and thanked her for coming.

"How 'bout some Glenn Miller?" he asked the band late in the evening, and they complied. Halfway through "Moonlight Serenade" he grabbed Gail's hand and led her out into the middle of the living room, took her in his arms and swayed her gently to the music. He could feel the eyes of all the guests on them and he hoped they were encouraged by this sight, by fate, that a marriage could be saved by a freak circumstance, by a simple mugging, by an instant of blinking in harsh light and not getting your name out of your mouth.

"This is great," he whispered to Gail.

"You're drunk," she said.

"Am not," he protested. "I just love you is all."

He felt her stiffen, and was aware she was looking behind him at something by the front door. He turned her casually, certain he was going to see the other man standing in the doorway over her shoulder, mocking him, and that he would mock right back; she was in his arms, after all, surrounded by witnesses, friends and family, thirty years of history. But as he began his victor's grin he saw that there was no one in the doorway, only the doorway, the doorway he had been forced to walk out of in October not because Gail had fallen in love with someone else, but because she was no longer in love with him. He had not just forgotten how to love her; they had forgotten how to love each other. And her memory, obviously, was far clearer on this issue than his. He could feel it in her breath, as it rose and fell against his healing ribs.

"Honey . . ." he started.

But she was restless in his arms, and their feet for a moment were tangled together so that they almost lost their footing, and he forgot what it was he was going to say.

"People will be leaving soon," she said. "It's getting late, Martin."

He pressed his lips gently to her forehead. "I know," he said.

WHO I WAS
SUPPOSED TO BE

I W A S twelve the summer I watched four men beat up my father on a softball field at his company picnic. My father was a little man with skinny white arms and a face which was usually pressed into an expression that would make you think he was trying to figure out a very complex math problem. He kept the books at West Rentz, and discovered one day that some of the company drivers were charging customers ten dollars extra for some bogus transportation fee on days that the drivers wanted to go out and drink beer after their shifts. My father reported it to Mr. Tom West himself and the four men were suspended without pay for two weeks, prompting the other employees to start a betting pool on when my father would get his.

It was near the end of the day, the sixth inning of the second game. My father and I had been sitting on the sidelines drinking sodas and watching when, at the end of the half inning, a couple guys started yelling up at him to come on down and get in the game. My father looked behind him, then to me.

"Me?" he yelled.

"Come on down," they said.

He looked at me again, nervous, and, I could tell, a little excited. I figured my father hadn't played a sport since we had thrown horseshoes on vacation a few years before.

"Can my son play too?" he yelled back. He winked at me.

The players had a little meeting. They looked worried, I thought, as if I could be any worse than my father.

"He's got a strong arm," my father called.

They waved us down.

They put him at catcher for the blue team. I didn't say anything, but I knew that you always put the wimpiest guy at catcher because in slow pitch the catcher doesn't even have to catch the ball; he just has to pick it up after the batter swings and misses and toss it back to the pitcher. My father was taking it all pretty seriously, though, because after eight years of company picnics this was the first time they'd ever asked him to play. I was at shortstop, turning red every time my father squatted down behind the plate and yelled, "Whoa batta, hey batta, wing it in here pitcha!" I saw some of the other men on the team laughing, and I was ashamed.

In the seventh and final inning one big guy on the red team got up and smacked a triple down the right field line. I looked over at him standing on third base and, seeing him viciously chewing on a huge wad of gum and glaring at my father, figured he was probably one of the suspended drivers, that the suspension didn't extend to being left out of the company picnic. The next guy up poked a little looper to the right of the pitcher, right at me, and out of the corner of my eye I saw the man on third break for home. I figured even if my father were so bad that he couldn't catch the ball that he would have time to run back to the backstop, pick it up, and tag the fat man out before he came chugging into home. I snagged the ball and threw it. My father was standing a few feet behind the plate, looking confused. He took his eye off the throw to check the runner and the ball glanced off the heel of his glove, just as the fat man swerved out of the baseline and ran him down. My father hit the ground with a thud, and then jumped up and tagged the fat man with his empty glove. The driver turned and socked my father in the face. One man leapt off the blue bench and charged at the two men.

Then two men from our outfield came plowing in, and, assuming it was a fair red versus blue fight, the rest of the men formed a little circle around the fight, as if they were seventh graders, cheering. I stood outside the circle, knowing I was the only one who knew it wasn't three against two but four, the drivers, against one, my father. I started pushing my way through the spectators with every intention of getting into the middle of the fight, but when I reached the front row all I could do was say, "Hey, stop. Hey, wait a minute," in a squeaky voice. There were things running through my mind that had something to do with letting my father fight his own battles, but even then I knew the real reason I didn't jump in was that I was scared, watching these big men pound on the thing at the bottom of the pile. I couldn't see, then, what good me throwing one punch was going to do when I would only end up in the same shape as my father, whose hand I saw for a moment breaking from the bottom of the pile and grabbing onto one of the driver's beards. I looked up into the stands for help and saw Tom West on the top tier, craning his neck like he was trying to get a better view. He took a drink from his beer and when he saw me looking up at him he took a couple of steps down toward the field.

About this time it became obvious to the rest of the men that there were four guys pummeling one guy who was already not moving. A few of them moved in and pulled the pile apart, careful not to piss any of the drivers off too badly, and the drivers, seeming satisfied that things were now even, went away cracking their knuckles and brushing the dust off their T-shirts. My father was lying facedown in the dirt. Somebody tipped him over onto his back with the toe of a sneaker. There was glass in his eyes, dirt stuffed up his nose, and blood and dust between his teeth.

My mother arrived at the hospital after I had been sitting in a sky blue waiting room for almost an hour, in the company of an old man who was watching *Hollywood Squares* and looking like he was about to cry the whole time. Like my father, my mother was little too, but she was that tough, compact kind of little that my father had never been able to achieve.

"Eddie?" I could hear the voice coming closer, hear the click of her boots on the hospital floor. "Eddie . . ."

I stood and the old man looked up at me, his eyes dazed and waiting, as if I could tell him something. My mother came charging into the room.

"Jesus, Eddie," she said, a cloud of smoke puffing from her mouth. There were always puffs of smoke coming out of my mother's mouth, with every syllable she spoke. Even when she didn't have a cigarette in her hand you could almost see the smoke hanging in front of her face because you were so used to it.

"He's still in there," I said. "Nobody's said anything to me."

"Bastards," she said, gripping the filter of her cigarette so tightly between her middle and index fingers that I thought she might crush it. "Those bastards." She put her hand up to my face, the cigarette inches from my bangs. "Did they hurt you?" she asked. "Did they hold you down?"

I took this as an accusation and started to cry. The old man got up and hurried out of the room.

"My baby," my mother said. "Those bastards."

The doctor, a black man with a short beard, came in. He told us that my father had a broken nose, three broken ribs, and glass chips in his left eye, as well as lots of other cuts and bruises.

"He'll need some dental work," the doctor added. "Physical therapy. More work on the eye." The man smiled at my mother reassuringly. "He'll be fine after a little R and R," he said.

At this I saw the air go out of my mother. She already worked five nights a week and Saturdays as a bartender at a local hotel lounge. She was hoping to cut that down too, I knew.

"We were getting it together," she said to the doctor, as if this would change things. The smoke wasn't puffing out of her now. It was trailing out from the corners of her mouth.

•

My father came home after three days in the hospital and my mother started working behind the hotel reservations desk during the day and stayed behind the bar at night. It was July and I was mowing lawns for summer money, but it seemed as though there were more twelve-year-old boys than there were lawns, so I wasn't making much. I told my mother I would get a job, told her I could deliver papers or walk dogs or sweep floors, but she said it was probably best for my job to be to keep my father company.

"No, really," I said. "I wouldn't mind."

She looked at me suspiciously. "What's so bad about hanging around here all day?"

"But we need the money."

She got it then. "I think there are a lot worse things than spending a few weeks at home with your father," she said. She was smiling but I knew she was mad. "He's been through the mill," she said. "But he's going to make it. He's going to go back to work in a few weeks and show everybody what kind of man he is."

"But Mom . . ." I said.

"Including you," she said.

"Joanna . . ." my father called out from the bedroom.

She turned toward the noise and then back at me. "I think you've got it pretty good, mister," she hissed, smoke exploding from her mouth in little shots right up my nose. "You don't have to clean up strangers' puke on bathroom floors, now do you?"

This was my mother's stock defense for everything, because one time, *one time*, she had to clean up one of the bathroom stalls in the hotel after some man threw up in it. In a moment of weakness she once admitted that the man wasn't even drunk— he had the flu or something—but my mother liked to portray her job as being the put-upon bartendress in the sleaziest bar in town. After I had been there once and seen the tourists she served cocktails to I stopped paying attention to her stories.

I didn't think of us as being poor. There were kids at my school who had dirty hair and clothes that were too big and brought apples in their brown bag lunches for dessert instead of Snac-Pac chocolate pudding and that was what poor meant to me. We lived in a one-story house that was smoky and sometimes cramped, but my father kept all the magazines stacked in neat piles and never threw his coat across the arm of the couch like most people do, so the house gave off the appearance of being orderly at least. We all shared one bathroom, which my mother complained about, but which I knew in a way she kind of liked because it meant that we all had to see each other in the morning, that sometimes she was washing her face and I was brushing my teeth and my father was shaving and there was something about that kind of togetherness that surpassed sitting around the dining room table.

The bathroom was the only place I smoked. I didn't even like smoking very much, didn't like the way it smelled on my mother when she kissed me good-bye or the way it made my mouth feel cloudy and dirty, but I liked to watch myself smoke. I did it most often on the days when I started feeling like my father, days when the cool kids at school would call me a nerd or a faggot, or times when I felt like the only girls who would ever like me were the fat, whiny ones who had already had braces for three years. Those days I would go home and, if my mother was working the happy hour shift and I had the house to myself, put on the rattiest undershirt I could find and the mirrored sunglasses that I kept in my underwear drawer. I'd stand in front of the bathroom mirror, light a cigarette with an easy, fluid motion, slowly inhale until the cigarette was lit, and then take long, deep drags, blowing the smoke back at my reflection in even, snaky streams, never taking my eyes off the guy in the mirror, the guy who nobody messes with, the guy who people stand aside to let walk by. I'd talk, the cigarette hanging in the corner of my mouth. I'd say things like: "What the fuck is that supposed to mean?" or "And who the hell are you supposed to be?"

•

I took half a sandwich in to my father at lunchtime. He was wearing boxer shorts and his stomach was wrapped in stiff white bandages. He had a tan patch over one eye. His other eye was staring up at the ceiling.

"Lunchtime," I said.

He turned his head and smiled. "There he is," he said. Two of his teeth were missing and his bottom lip was stitched all the way across. He looked like a psychopath, I thought. Like a psychopathic nerd, though, with his pale, skinny legs sticking out of the boxer shorts and his hair straight and combed neatly to one side.

"I thought maybe you'd gone out," he said. "I didn't hear you."

"I thought maybe you were sleeping," I said, handing him the limp bologna on white sandwich on a napkin and a Spider-Man tumbler full of orange juice. I stood there and watched him take a bite. I had hardly spoken to him since the picnic. He was taking painkillers and spent most of his time in a deep sleep. He cringed a little when he bit down into the bread.

"Mom left some green Jell-O," I said, "if it's too hard."

He shook his head, chewing deliberately and swallowing the bite down in an awkward gulp. "This is nothing," he said. "Try biting down on some ape-man's fist."

"No thanks," I said.

"Sit," he said. "Talk to me."

I pulled up a chair next to the bed, like we were still in a cold hospital room. He had mayonnaise on his lip and I almost reached for the napkin to wipe it off but I couldn't do it.

"What are you up to?" he asked.

"Sittin' here," I said.

He smiled. The stitches on his lip stretched.

Years before I had sat with my father at the dining room table and run an unsharpened pencil down the figures in one of his ledger books. When he took off his wire-rimmed glasses to rub his eyes I would put them on and hold them up on my nose with one hand while I made imaginary marks with my free hand. I believed that the marks my father made in his ledger books altered the universe, that the numbers were more than figures on U-Hauls and color televisions.

"Have you eaten?" he asked me. He had finished his sandwich and the mayonnaise on his lip was gone.

"I had one too," I said.

"You know what bologna's made out of, Ed?"

"What?"

"Pig guts," he said. "Intestines."

"It is not," I said.

"Look on the package," he said. "It says it right there. *Pig guts.*"

I wanted to ask him what it was like to be beaten, if he remembered being under the pile, if he had looked up and seen me standing there.

"You want some more juice?" I asked instead.

"No," he said. "Don't worry about me. I'm okay."

"Sure," I said. I shifted. I wanted out.

"Well," he said, sighing. It was the point that we had always reached after a few minutes together in those years. The ongoing horror of junior high social classes had made me desperately afraid that my father would rub off on me, that if we had discussions that went beyond how are you, I'm fine, that I would start thinking the way he thought, start being who he was, start wanting to get out the old ledger books and sit at the kitchen table poring over meaningless figures when out in the world the guy who I was supposed to be was looking at his watch, getting impatient, thinking I was never going to show.

I took the damp napkin and went to get him some more orange juice even though he didn't want it. When I came back his unbandaged eye was closed, and I was relieved. Only another thousand or so conversations to dodge, I figured, before I was grown up.

My mother got the night off from the bar and arrived home at five o'clock with three crossword puzzle books and an industrial-size bottle of wine under her arm.

"I know what you've been up to," she said to me, setting the things on the dining room table. "The two of you, moping around all day. I've got a night off and I'm going to enjoy it."

"Crossword puzzles," I said. "Yea."

She smiled. "I'm so pleased you've reached that smart ass stage," she said. "I was worried there for a while." She set the puzzles off to the side and put the wine in the middle of the table. "The books are for tomorrow when I'm gone. Tonight we're having a blowout party."

"Uh oh," my father said. He had gotten up and was standing in the doorway. He had put on a pair of blue sweatpants and an undershirt. I thought if I replaced his wire-rims with my mirrors that he wouldn't look half bad, what with his face all messed up. "What's the occasion?"

"It's the annual time-to-get-this-family-back-on-its-feet party," my mother said, flitting around the kitchen putting away groceries. She had the gift of making brutal honesty sound like the lightest comment ever made. I had seen it before, and I knew all the signs. Anytime she was too happy I knew she was panicking.

An hour later we sat down to spaghetti and the jug of red wine. My mother tuned in to some station on the radio that played old songs that made my father smile. He was propped up on pillows on an easy chair that we had pulled to the table, and he held his plate on his lap and balanced his glass of wine on the arm of the chair. My mother poured a glass of wine for herself and then half of one for me. Up until that point my drinking experience had been limited to a glass of wine on the Thanksgiving before and two beers with my cousin on the Fourth of July when I was ten.

"It really is a party," I said.

"You bet," she said, winking at me, like it was all part of a surprise that I was supposed to be clued in on. "Any guy who takes care of his father should get a little reward at the end of a day."

My father raised his glass to that one, as if I had knocked myself out tending to his every want and need. We ate the spaghetti and I sipped my wine slowly, making faces into my napkin after every sip because I thought it tasted terrible but I didn't want them to know it. They weren't paying much attention, though. By the time they finished eating they had both finished their third glass.

My mother looked up at me and smiled. Then she put her paper napkin over her plate and poured herself another glass of wine. She pulled the table back from my father and his easy chair and my plate moved about two feet to my left. There was a soul song on the radio, some woman with a throaty voice singing about doing it slow and moaning between lyrics. My mother picked up the plate off my father's lap and refilled his glass. She was swaying back and forth to the music and staring at my father. Then she reached out and took both his hands and pulled him into a standing position. He grunted. I gave up on my spaghetti and poured another glass of wine for myself, watching them move out into the middle of the room. My mother put her arms around my father's neck and rocked him back and forth. I drank my wine and watched them dance and smile at each other. My father closed his uncovered eye and my mother reached to the table for her glass of wine. Another song came on and my parents didn't seem to notice. They just kept on dancing. Then my father leaned forward and kissed my mother's neck. She tilted her head back, holding her wine behind his head, and I saw his stitched lips come apart as he bit her throat. I drank another glass of wine. They had both stopped moving, my father with his face pressed against her, my mother with her head back and her eyes closed. I sat at the kitchen table and heard a mower start up outside. The sun was setting and it came through the window behind me and burned the back of my neck. My parents stood there for a good two minutes and I thought that they might stand there forever, that I might sit at the table watching them forever, and that the sun would rise and set July into August and the three of us would never know the difference.

The doorbell rang. They both opened their eyes and looked at each other, startled, as if they had just met and had become much too intimate much too fast. Then she pulled away from him and he lost his balance and fell against the television, catching himself before he hit the floor. I stood up to help and my head floated off my body, never, I imagined, to be heard from again. My father had regained some semblance of a standing position, was holding on to the TV watching my mother answer the door. It was Tom West.

"This is an unexpected surprise," my mother said.

Tom West looked around. He was probably ten years younger than my father and looked like he was made of plastic, like he was constantly standing in front of a video camera filming one of his cheesy local commercials. He had never been to our house before and I saw him look at the table, past the wine bottle at me. He winked.

"Hey, sport," he said, and I giggled.

He ignored me and nodded to my father. "I need to talk some business," he said, in such a way that it was clear that he didn't mean to speak to my father about figures.

"Sit down," my father said. I could tell he was in pain from being slung against the television by my mother.

"Thanks, no," Tom West said. He looked at my mother, then back at my father. "Maybe privately," he said.

"Oh no," my mother said. "Fuck you, mister." My father and I looked at her, shocked. Tom West smiled as if my mother had just made a joke.

"What is it?" my father said to Tom West, after staring down my mother as best he could.

Tom West sighed, looked sideways at my mother. "I've just come from a meeting with a man by the name of Harold Norton," he said. "Harold and I are becoming partners. As a result . . ." He paused and glanced warily over at my mother again. "Well, as a result, there are going to be a lot of changes."

"Okay," my father said seriously. "The doctors say it will only be another week or so."

"Harold seems to believe," Tom West said, "that between the two of us, he and I, we can take care of the books."

"That's a full-time job," my father said. His hand slipped off the edge of the television and he swung his arms around in circles, trying to keep his balance, like somebody on the edge of a pool. Tom West grabbed his shoulder and steadied him.

"You aren't the only one," Tom West continued, as if he hadn't just saved my father from putting his arm through the TV screen. "I've got several calls to make tonight."

"Several calls bullshit," my mother said. She turned to my father. "Don't listen to him," she said. "Don't you see what he's doing?" Her words were slightly slurred from anger and wine and her eyes were slits.

"Joanna," my father said.

"Of course any references you need . . ." Tom West said. "I have no doubt that you'll have no trouble . . ."

"I don't think you understand the time involved in this," my father said. "It's not an easy job."

"I'm certain it isn't," Tom West said. "Harold seems—"

"Fuck Harold," my mother said. She grabbed on to Tom West's blue oxford shirt and turned him toward her. "There is no Harold," my mother said. "What do you take us for?"

In silence, Tom West peeled my mother's white fingers one at a time from around his shirtsleeve. When he had freed himself he said, "Mrs. Logan, I understand you're upset. Let's not let this get ugly."

"Joanna," my father said. He started walking toward the front door. I had an image of him pulling a pistol out of his bandage and blowing Tom West away. I wondered what we would all do then.

Instead, he opened the front door and motioned for Tom West to follow him out, then closed the door behind them. My mother turned to me, furious. I let my head rest against the back window. I closed my eyes, keeping them open in narrow slits just enough to see her. She stood there steaming.

"I should have seen it coming sooner," she said. "It's been just a little too long since he let somebody screw him."

I burped. I didn't know what language my mother was speaking.

"Eddie," she said. "Eddie, are you drunk?"

I got this idea into my head then: none of this was really happening; I wasn't really me and she wasn't really her and my father wasn't really standing on the front porch shaking hands with the man who had just fired him. I smiled at my mother and let myself think that she was pretty, comforted by the thought that we were all just figments of my drunken imagination.

My mother snapped up her cigarettes and went into their bedroom, slammed the door hard enough to shake the chair I was sitting on. Through the window I saw the headlights of Tom West's car light up our driveway, then the sound of tires on gravel. I wondered for a moment if my father had gone with him. But then the door opened and my father stood there in the doorway, regarding his home as if he had heard a lot about it but was now actually seeing it for the first time.

"Where's your mother?" he asked, when his eyes reached me.

"She went to bed," I said.

He eased the door closed, sat down in the easy chair with his back to me.

"There are better jobs out there anyway, Eddie," he said.

I hiccuped. "Lots better jobs," I said.

"Maybe I could play professional ball," he said. "What'dya think, Ed? We could all travel with the team, see the country, leave this house behind."

"Sounds good," I said. "I bet Mom would like you in uniform."

He turned around, smiled. "You think?" he said, for a moment believing the whole thing. It was his trick, I knew then; it was what swept him through this kind of night. He rode on a wake of hoarded individual moments when anything seemed possible.

"Sure she would," I said. "She'd love it."

●

When I woke up in the morning she was already gone to work. I looked in on my father and saw him asleep on his stomach, his bruised face buried in the pillow. I put on a torn black undershirt and my sunglasses, then went out into the living room to get one of my mother's cigarettes. The plates were still on the table, the spaghetti hard and stuck to them. The empty jug of wine was lying on its side against my plate. I took a cigarette out of an open pack on the kitchen counter and went into the bathroom and swung the door partway closed, so I could hear my father if he called for me. I lit the cigarette and blew the smoke at my reflection.

"Another fuckin' hangover," I said. "Another fuckin' bottle of whiskey floating around in there."

My father stumbled through the door, pushed past me and knelt down and threw up a chunk of something into the toilet. I stood over him and put the cigarette behind my back. "God," I said, when he looked up at me, and a puff of smoke came out of my mouth.

"Eddie," my dad said. He wiped his mouth clean with a piece of toilet paper and rubbed his hands over his face, trying to peel the hangover off. "Eddie, what the hell are you doing?" His hair was mussed and his undershirt was wrinkled.

"Nothing," I said through the smoke. "Standin' here."

He got up and went back out of the bathroom. I flushed the cigarette and looked at the guy in the mirror for some pointers, but the guy in the mirror never had a father he'd had to explain things to, so he didn't have a thing to say.

My father came back into the bathroom with the rest of the pack of cigarettes and his prescription sunglasses. He picked up mine off the sink and fit them onto my head. Then he put his on, the one lens covering all but a thin circle of the patch over his left eye. He lit a cigarette and handed it to me, then lit one for himself. We looked into the mirror at each other.

"Hey," I said. I giggled, trying to be the guy but being me because I was embarrassed.

"Hey, yourself," he said. He looked as mean as any guy I'd ever seen. "Giggling like a goddamn girl. Who the fuck are you?"

I stopped smiling. "You got some balls talking to me like that," I said. "Who the fuck are you?"

He didn't answer. Everything was quiet. There was smoke trailing out from my father's broken nose, and he licked his dry stitched lips until they were wet. He had a slight smirk on his face. Through the fog we scrutinized the guys in the mirror.

RETIREMENT

a L F R E D was out of Pepto-Bismol. After dinner he slapped furiously at the base of the bottle, removed his eyeglasses and peered into the pink-crusted hole. Empty. Bewildering, this shortsightedness, after so many years. He weighed the empty bottle in his hand. A trip to the pharmacy was out of the question. If Mr. Wayne arrived home to find the house empty . . . then what? What might he say? My apologies, sir, I had to rush out for a bottle of antacid to soothe my stomach. And then the whole shameful tale would be revealed. You're making me ill, Mr. Wayne, he would say. I worry, I hardly sleep, I'm an old man, can't shoulder this burden any longer. No, he could not tell Mr. Wayne, and he could not leave the house.

Alfred went into the parlor and sank down in the easy chair, moaned softly, held his stomach with both hands like a little boy.

I could falter at any—

He shook the thought away. If he could relax, focus his mind elsewhere, he would be all right. He turned on the television. Men in suits were running down a fire escape, their dress shoes clacking on the metal steps. They leapt to the street where a man with a gold tooth stood, pointing a large gun, which he then fired into the men's chests. On the next channel, an antelope was being pulled to pieces by a cougar. Alfred moved on. A woman fought for balance on the edge of a building, swung her arms around frantically, plummeted to the street. Alfred shut off the television, burped.

He knew many men who would in a moment trade places with him. It should have been a simple life—*and wasn't it once?*—even glamorous: a flourish when answering the door, a touch of respectful evasiveness, cigar and brandy at the ready for Mr. Wayne when he arrived home, perhaps some stimulating conversation, a friendly game of chess, insight to a riddle from the Riddler.

It was torture. Every hour, in every corner of the miserable world, devious plots were being hatched to kill Batman. This indisputable fact had always been of minor concern to Mr. Wayne, but with each passing year loomed larger and deeper in Alfred's heart. The concept of a world without the Caped Crusader was, frankly, not what distressed him so. No, his fear was that he might sleep through it, or panic and falter at the moment of crisis, that, with his resolve waning by the hour, he would not be capable of acting with the decisiveness an urgent situation would demand.

The telephone rang. Alfred lifted himself out of his easy chair. "Wayne Manor," he announced into the mouthpiece.

There was a brief silence, then the line went dead. Alfred's hand trembled. This was surely it. Someone had discovered the secret, someone was watching the house. Soon, a car would pull up out front, several criminals would emerge. Before he could trigger the alarm they would overpower him, lock him in the pantry. They would wait for Mr. Wayne to return, and Alfred would be gagged and bound, utterly helpless.

He went into the kitchen, tidied up, threw the empty bottle of Pepto-Bismol into the trash. He prepared himself a cup of chamomile tea. Just as he took his first sip, he heard a woman's voice in the front yard. Raucous laughter, then a key in the lock.

"Alfred!"

The familiar voice, the usual greeting. He emptied his tea into the sink and scurried to the foyer. Mr. Wayne was carrying a large woman over his shoulder. The woman was slapping Mr. Wayne on the back of his legs and shrieking. Her skirt was askew and Alfred could see her underpants pinching her heavy thighs.

"Any calls?" Mr. Wayne asked. He was breathing hard and sweat beaded his temples.

"Any calls!" the woman echoed, then burst into laughter.

"No sir," Alfred said. He briefly considered reporting the hang-up, but then dismissed it, knowing that Mr. Wayne would dismiss it as soon as it was mentioned. Or, worse yet, make one of his comments. You're getting paranoid in your old age, Alfred, he might say.

The woman looked at Alfred through the crook of Mr. Wayne's elbow. Her face was bright red. She appeared to be somewhere in her forties—a bit older than the usual selection—but upside down as she was, Alfred found it difficult to distinguish her actual age.

"Guess what we've been doing?" she asked.

Alfred answered with a slightly raised eyebrow, indicating mild interest but no judgment.

"Time for bed, dear," Mr. Wayne said. He tossed a wink at Alfred and carried the woman up the stairs to the second floor. She waved as they went, her long black hair brushing the carpeted steps.

Some time early in the morning Alfred started awake from fitful drowsing, sat up in bed in his little room off the kitchen, certain that he heard someone milling about. He put on his eyeglasses and crept across his room, opened the door. He saw the woman, wrapped in a sheet from Mr. Wayne's bed, standing at the refrigerator, taking stock of its contents.

"Shall I make you a snack?" he offered.

She turned, unsurprised that he should be there.

"I was after some wine," she said.

He tightened the sash on his robe and joined her at the refrigerator. The cool blast from inside made the hair on his legs prickle. The kitchen was dark and hot and, fresh from half-sleep, the chill to his skin was so pleasant that for a moment he was certain he was dreaming.

"How long have you been here, Alfred?"

"Thirty-one years," he said. He turned to face her, saw that she was even older than he had first thought, perhaps fifty, nearly Mr. Wayne's age. The excitement of the night worn off, the wrinkles around her eyes were profound. She looked rather grandmotherly, even, heavy as she was, a woman one would seek out for comfort.

"In those thirty-one years," she whispered, "has anyone ever poured you a glass of wine?"

"I don't recall," he said.

"Then I shall be the one you recall."

She turned him away from the refrigerator and led him to the kitchen table. A moment later she placed a crystal glass of white wine and the bottle in front of him and—taking a moment to adjust the sheet around her—took the chair opposite his and sipped from her own glass.

"My father was a butler," she said. "We lived in St. Louis."

He smiled politely. "A beautiful city."

"You've been there?"

"No," he admitted.

She set her glass on the table. "It's a terrible place. It smells of beer and rats and in the summer men sit on their porches wearing nothing but underwear."

"I grew up in London," he said suddenly.

"London," she mused. "Now there's a wonderful place."

"You know it?"

"No," she said.

"As a boy I dreamed of working in Buckingham Palace," he said. "I imagined I would be the one to wake the king in the morning." He blushed, embarrassed to have given so much away. "Of course many boys had that dream."

"You've done well," she said. "Not the king. But Batman."

He paused for an instant, then fixed his seasoned gaze of puzzlement upon her. "I'm afraid I don't follow you," he said, but even as he uttered the words—this oft-practiced denial—he felt the chill on his legs again, felt his skin tingle, and the sensation was no less pleasurable than it had been before.

"I'm going to let some people into the house in a few minutes," she said. "I thought you should know."

"Indeed," he said. And act, he thought. Know, then act. This was his moment, finally, his chance; he was perfectly composed, in complete authority of his senses. But how many times had he woken Mr. Wayne, groggy from drinking and sex, with legitimate concerns, and how many times had he been dismissed with the wave of a hand and a roll of the eyes?

"Have another," the woman said, filling his glass.

It was not happening in a blur, as he always imagined it would. Each decisive moment arrived and departed with a clarity of its own, and he deliberately and serenely allowed each to pass. For the first time in months, years perhaps, he felt peace, the control of this inevitable situation finally and completely within his grasp.

"Miss?"

"Yes, Alfred?"

"It will be swift?"

She smiled gently. "Relatively," she said.

He nodded. "All right then."

She left him alone in the kitchen. He sat sipping his wine in the dark, and after a few moments he heard noises from the back of the house. He had imagined these sounds many times, heard them waking and sleeping so often, that now they were only a comfort to him as he rose from the table and gently, silently *so as not to disturb a thing* rinsed the faint stain of lipstick from the rim of the crystal glass.

GRAVITY

I T rained the morning of the day we killed Dennis Zeller. It came steady; we woke up to it beating on the wooden roofs of our cabins and ran to breakfast in the camp cafeteria with jackets covering our heads. The sixth-grade trip up the mountain that was planned for that day was postponed. Instead, we had to sit in the arts and crafts room, pasting leaves to construction paper, making nature collages. My best friend Jessica and I sat at a table by the window, watching the rain slap against the glass. Behind us, Dennis Zeller shot acorns out of his mouth at the backs of our heads, grabbed at Jessica's long blond braid, and whispered his usual taunts.

"Hey geek boy. It ain't romance till you get in her pants."

The rain slowed by late afternoon. The girls went back to their side of the camp to change into their outdoor gear while the boys played kill-the-man-with-the-ball on the lawn in front of the cafeteria. I sat on the grass, far from the game, watching a woolly caterpillar crawl up my leg. Dennis Zeller didn't play either. He kicked rocks around and glared at the boys. He was aching, I knew, to get into it.

The climb up the mountain was long and wet; we carried walking sticks partly to balance us and partly to feel like real adventurers. Jessica and I had a sword fight with ours, jabbing and dodging, laughing and tripping over ourselves and each other on the muddy slope, while the rest of the group trudged on ahead.

In the grayness just before nightfall, Dennis Zeller stood staring up into a tree where a snake was curled around a small branch. The other kids were moving on; someone had discovered a fossil and everyone was headed in that direction, their backs turned away from us. Jessica held me back, grabbed my arm and pointed to Dennis, then made a pushing motion and giggled. I snuck up and squatted behind him, pretending to be looking for something, and tied his shoe laces together—not tight even, just in a simple bow. He wasn't paying attention. He had his hand out toward the snake like Tarzan, willing it to come to him. I scampered away on my hands and knees, behind a tree.

"Hey Dennis," Jessica said, walking toward him.

"Shut up," he said. "Can't you see—"

That's when she gave him the shove, the one that was supposed to be tiny, just enough to send him sprawling into the mud, to splat so loud that all the other kids would turn around and laugh at the fool, but she slipped on the wet ground and ran her whole body into him. Trying to get his footing, Dennis went stumbling toward the edge of the hill, not to the path that we had come from, but to a drop-off where you could see the tops of trees from where we stood. He swung his arms around wildly, seemed to almost rock there for a second on the edge of the bluff, and then tumbled without a sound. Jessica stood there, frozen, and as I reached her I could see Dennis Zeller bounce against a tree branch and hit the ground, watched him slide from rock to tree like some crazy sledder, until he finally came to a stop a hundred yards below us.

The light was disappearing over the trees. No one saw Dennis go, no one but Jessica and me. She turned to me and for one second I thought she would go down after him. Then she started screaming, "Dennis fell! Dennis fell!" and people far ahead of us turned back, voices rose out of the woods. I felt my arm rise up,

my index finger slowly uncurl itself from my fist to point toward
the bluff. The forest guide rushed over, took one look down, and
then we were all rushed away down the path by the teenage
counselors. They took us down the hill to the cafeteria, put on a
movie, *Where the Red Fern Grows,* and left us there. The class
crowded around Jessica and me, wanting to know what had happened, wanting to know if Dennis Zeller had jumped, if he had
slipped, if he was dead. Jessica took my arm and pulled me out of
the cafeteria. We ran around the side of the building and sat
down behind the trash dumpster, hiding from the other kids. Her
knees were shaking.

"It's okay," I told her. "It's all right. Nobody saw." I squeezed
her arm, something that I had never done before, something that
I thought my father might do to my mother if they got themselves in such a situation.

"His shoes," she whispered. "They'll see his shoes and they'll
know." Her eyes were halfway closed, as if she were in pain, but
she wasn't crying. It struck me at that moment that in six years I
had never seen her cry once. Her face was like an old picture; it
never changed, never gave much of her away.

"I'll do it," I said, because it was Jessica, always, who was the
leader, and I wanted to be in charge for once. "I'll take care of it."

I made the half-mile hike up the mountain, thinking of stories
I could tell, reasons why Dennis Zeller might tie his own
shoelaces together. It was dark now, crisp in the March air. I left
the path and made my way through the woods until I could see
lights bobbing around on the hillside, counselors with flashlights
crowded around the tree that Dennis lay by. They stood over
him, four or five of them. One of the girls was crying, and a man,
the guide who had looked down the hill after it happened,
looked as if he were about to faint.

I went toward them slowly. They were staring down at the
body, silently, and I was able to get to the edge of their circle
without them seeing me. I meant to look at his feet first, at his
feet only, but I could not, because he didn't look dead at all. His

mud-caked T-shirt was still tucked into his jeans, and his bare arms seemed unscathed. His jaw was set, his hair mussed but not torn. The only thing that looked dead were his eyes. They were wide open, huge and wild. They looked past the counselors and straight at me. They held me there, where I stood shivering in the mud.

I felt one of the counselors put a hand on my shoulder.

"Go on, Alex," he said. "There's nothing you can do here."

I lowered my eyes to Dennis Zeller's feet. He had on only one shoe. His left foot wore a torn and soiled sock.

"Alex . . ."

His right shoe was untied, the laces muddy but intact.

"Go on, get out of here. . . ."

The counselor gave me a shove back toward the path, and I ran through the woods, down to the cafeteria, where the movie went on, and the other kids had quieted down. Jessica, sitting near the door with her back to the screen, had stopped shaking. She stared ahead at the wall, her face blank, her eyes empty.

"We're covered," I said. "It's over."

Camp was called off. They loaded us back on the bus the next morning, only two days into what was supposed to be a week-long trip. We told the counselors our story, a story we didn't have to decide on but that just came to us together. Simple: we were standing there, minding our own business, and when we looked up he was falling off the bluff. There was no time to grab him, nothing we could do to help.

We returned to school and sat every afternoon for the next three days in the assembly room in a circle around the guidance counselors, who were supposed to help us through any torment we might be feeling. Jessica and I sat together, cross-legged, our knees touching. We were silent, didn't cough or rustle around even when the other kids started getting restless. We remained still, until the last of our classmates had headed out onto the playground after the bell. Only then did we rise from the hard floor, stretch our legs, and give each other the only thing that we would allow, a small smile of encouragement—we have made it through another day.

Jessica had lived three houses down from me since kindergarten, with her grandparents. We grew up together, ran naked through sprinklers in the summers and doubled up on the toboggan when the snow came. On our first day of second grade we were allowed to walk alone to school, then skipped, ran through the woods by town, her as the Lone Ranger and me as Tonto, tracking imaginary bad guys and pelting empty campsites with pencils and erasers from our backpacks. Everyone took us for brother and sister. We learned alike, both ahead of most everyone else. Jessica was the smartest of all; she made the top grades and won all the awards in our class. I tagged along right behind, always trying to catch up with her but never quite able to do it. Still, we were both in all the advanced groups. By fifth grade this, plus the fact that we were always together, made us backwards in the eyes of almost everyone, but especially Dennis Zeller, who used to throw rocks at us as we rode our bikes to school. Dennis was like this; it was in his nature, we all believed. Rumor had it that he hit his dog, a huge, frightening-looking mutt, with a baseball bat when it was bad. And Dennis would have been out of school except for one thing; he could sing like nobody's business, move across and over and all around a melody like he was born to do nothing else. He got all the starring roles in our school chorus performances, even when he was on probation or suspended. In music class, Tuesday and Thursday mornings right before lunch, you could hear his voice from the back row, moving through you, drowning you out. Hearing that voice you could never imagine that he could slash the seat of your bike with his pocket knife, or piss in your locker. And standing behind him on the risers as he sang his solos on assembly night, you could see the change in the faces of your own parents; this boy can't be so bad, this boy is an angel. The way the lights worked in the gym, you nearly could see a halo on Dennis Zeller's head, if you really tried.

Five days after the accident we returned to our regular classes. Nobody in our homeroom wanted to switch to Dennis's desk, so instead of leaving it empty there in the middle of the room our teacher moved it into the corner where it sat, Dennis's handwritten *fuck you* still visible to all of us.

After school I spent my time at Jessica's. Her grandmother had died the summer before, so she and her grandfather lived alone in the biggest house on the block. Mr. Higgins, her grandfather, had been paralyzed in the Korean War and got around in a wheelchair. After thirty years, he was so good at it he entertained us with wheelies on the kitchen tile and going backward down the porch stairs in front of the house. He loved Jessica. Her mother had dropped her off with him and his wife to babysit one afternoon when Jessica was barely a year and had never returned. He was a smart old man, and since Mrs. Higgins had died he would sit for hours with us in the sunroom, a beer in one hand and a cigarette in the other, going over long division and social studies, and telling us stories about the war. My parents both worked, my father during the day and my mother, who was a nurse, at night. I saw him at dinner and her at breakfast. We ate together on Sundays, usually in front of the television.

"You two are awful mopey," Mr. Higgins said, a week after we had returned from camp. "Sitting in here like a couple of rejects."

We were in the sunroom, drawing possible superheroes for a comic book we had talked about starting. Jessica was the artist, not me, and my prospective heroes always ended up looking like stick men with capes and boots.

"We're drawing, Grampa," Jessica said. "Not moping."

"Looks like moping to me." He twirled himself around and leaned down in his chair to get a better look at our work.

"That's a silly-looking guy, Alex," he said.

I put my hand over my paper. "I'm just messing around," I said. "I'm not really trying."

"Well try, boy," he said. "When I was on the line some kid comes up to me and says, 'I coulda shot him but I wasn't really trying.' What do you think I said?"

Jessica sighed. " 'That'd be fine as long as he isn't trying either,' " she said.

"Who told you that story?" Mr. Higgins said. "Who stole my story?" He sat back in his chair and lit a cigarette. He was bored, I knew. Sometimes Jessica and I wondered what he did all day when we were at school. I imagined him wheeling around the big house from room to room, taking stock of everything that was there.

"What's happened with that boy who died?" he asked.

Jessica looked at me, but didn't flinch a bit.

"What do you mean what's happened?" she said. "They buried him and now his desk's sitting in the corner."

"That's the boy who was always throwing stuff at you two," he said. "I remember that boy. Followed you home once and stood out in the driveway, scowling. Ugly as hell."

"Grampa, we're trying to work," Jessica said. She crumpled up a piece of paper and threw it across the room into the trash can.

"But he had that voice," Mr. Higgins said. "He sure could sing a song."

"Other people can sing too," I said. "I can sing. So can she. So can half the class, just maybe not as loud." I wanted to tell him then, just to tell somebody. Mr. Higgins always said something smart. I wanted to tell him and hear him say, "That's okay, these things happen all the time. . . . Nothing to get all bent out of shape about." But I kept quiet. Jessica was looking at me, and I knew that somehow she knew what I was thinking.

•

That Friday I spent the night at Jessica's. We camped out in the backyard. My father said it was the last time, that in seventh grade I wouldn't be able to sleep in the same tent with a girl and not think about certain things. Teenage boys weren't supposed to spend the night at girls' houses, he told me. Didn't I know that? And I did; it made sense for everyone but me and Jessica. I wanted to tell my father that Jessica was as safe from me as he himself would have been if we ever did anything like a camp-out. When I looked at her, I saw something that was untouchable, something that I had no business even thinking about.

We waited until we saw the light in Mr. Higgins's room go out. Then we snuck back into the house and got one beer from the refrigerator. It was tradition, something we had done since fourth grade. Jessica cracked it open while I got out a box of pow- dered sugar doughnuts from my overnight bag.

"It's so quiet," Jessica whispered. "Let's tell ghost stories."

"No way," I said.

She was quiet. She flung her ponytail back and made a face, then drank down some of the beer and let out a long, satisfied sigh.

"Alex," she said, leaning back against her pillow. "Are you gonna get married?"

"I don't know," I said. "Why?"

"If you get married, I bet some night you'll be lying in bed next to your wife and you'll tell her the whole thing. That's how you are. You tell everything. You can't help it."

"I'll never tell," I said. "I'll never tell anybody, not even if I get married. We'll go to jail."

"They don't put kids in jail," she said. "Worse, they make us go live with mean kids. Imagine a whole school full of Zellers. That's what we'd be living with."

"You're never gonna tell anybody?" I asked her.

"I might tell my husband," she said, and I saw her with a man, a stranger, better-looking and smarter than me. In my mind she was still twelve, but the man was old, thirty, and she held on tight to his arm, skipped along beside him down toward the marriage altar.

"I might tell him after a time," she said. "After seven years you can't arrest people for crimes. I looked it up over the weekend. When we're nineteen we can tell anybody we want."

"It was an accident," I said. "Not a crime."

"You think anybody's gonna buy that? No way." She shook her head, lay back on her sleeping bag. "Someday we'll make a movie about it and be famous," she said. She tilted the beer can over her mouth and let the last of it drip down, then wiped powdered sugar off her face with the sleeve of her jacket. She closed her eyes, but I kept sitting up, the flashlight in my lap, shining right on her face. I imagined him coming for us, him with those terrible eyes, scratching on the canvas of the tent.

Jessica opened her eyes. "Shut that thing off, Alex," she said. "How am I supposed to sleep with that shining in my face?"

"Sorry . . ." I shut the flashlight off and the darkness took me, covered both of us like a heavy shadow. I shivered, listened. He could have been sitting next to me, or worse yet, next to Jessica, and I never would have known it. I imagined feeling the touch of his hand on mine in the darkness. I knew that I would die from fear, that I could never protect Jessica from evil like that.

Every morning before school I threw up. The smell of breakfast would hit me as I was getting dressed and it was always too much for my stomach. I learned to clean up after myself, to get sick without crying, to wipe my own face and wash the bathroom tile without the help of my mother, who would always comment that I looked pale as I sat down at the breakfast table but then go on to talk about something else. It became hard to sleep too. I would be awake when my mother came in at midnight, listen at my door to her and my father talking quietly in their bedroom across the hall.

"He never talks to me anymore," I heard my father say one night. "I barely see him. He comes home from the Higginses' and sits up in his room."

"He's growing up," my mother said. "That's all. He's thinking more."

My father said something I couldn't hear. I opened my bedroom door and crept into the hall and to their door.

"He doesn't have any friends besides her," I heard my father say. He was whispering now, as if he knew I was out there, listening. "It was one thing a few years ago. But they're almost thirteen years old, for God's sake. He needs to hang out with some boys. Needs to branch out a little bit."

"It's that age," my mother said. "It's that age when everything is scary."

I went back into my room and lay down, stared at the ceiling and tried to make myself believe that my mother was right, that even things like what happened to Dennis Zeller stopped being scary when you got old enough, that there would be a time when I would be able to slip off to sleep without thinking of him, when I would be able to look at Jessica and not see her feet going out from under her and her slamming into him, and him, teetering, always teetering, at that edge.

Spring came in full and our whole class became restless with the thought of summer. Dennis Zeller's desk was covered with spring projects, had become a display table for some of our Civil War dioramas. Every day in class I would catch myself looking at it, watching shoe box battles being fought by tiny soldiers where Dennis had once dug holes with scissors into the shiny wood and yawn the huge, gaping yawns that we all felt but no one else dared show.

Jessica and I continued to work on our comic book, sitting in the sunroom of her grandfather's house, watching the green spread from the grass to the trees. Some days I wondered if she had forgotten, if Dennis, like a dreary day, was something that had passed for her long ago.

I became the writer of the comic book and she took over all the drawing. We had finally decided on our hero. He was an androgynous creature, a strange mix of tiger, hawk, and man, who not only had super strength but could also swim underwater for days and fly as long, fast, and high as he wanted to, Superman and Aquaman combined. The hitch was that he could lose his powers easily if he thought about them. If he was swimming with sharks through an old pirate shipwreck in the middle of the Pacific and then thought, I'm a man, I can't swim, then he would begin gasping for breath and have to get one of his ocean friends to take him to the surface. At the end of our first issue this happened while he was flying, chasing after an airplane that had lost its wing and was spiraling, out of control and raging with flames.

"That's a real idea you got there," Mr. Higgins said. "Power of the mind. What's going to happen to the old coot?"

"It's a secret," I said.

"He's going to fall and get squished, Grampa," Jessica said. "What do you think?"

"I think you're growing up too fast, is what I think," he said. "The both of you." He popped a wheelie and swung his chair around in a circle. I laughed.

"Some day while we're at school you're gonna flip that thing over and crack your head open," Jessica said. "It's only a matter of time, you know."

Mr. Higgins got quiet, reached for his beer on the floor and sipped at it.

"What's the matter with you, darlin'?" he asked. He looked from her to me.

"We're trying to finish our book," she said.

"He's still in the middle of falling," I said.

"That," Mr. Higgins said, "reminds me of something I heard as a boy, something we used to talk about over in the trenches when we were getting our butts shot at. I don't know if you can use it or not, but it might give you something to think about."

"We already know what's going to happen," Jessica said.

"Just wait a minute," he said. "Listen to this. One time, a long time ago, there was this Indian who fell off a bridge. The bridge was hundreds of feet up in the air and below it was nothing but rocks. So that Indian's falling along and what do you think he did?"

"Pretended he could fly," I said. "Just like our guy."

"Nope," Mr. Higgins said.

"Landed on a stack of mattresses that just happened to be sitting there," Jessica said.

"Nope, Miss Smarty-pants," he said. "He didn't do a thing. Didn't make a noise. Didn't call for help. You know why?"

A wave of nausea passed through me, up my stomach and into my throat. I looked at Jessica. I wished that Mr. Higgins was dead and that Jessica and I were married, living in the old house, drawing pictures in the sunroom and not afraid of anything.

"He didn't yell cause he passed out," Jessica said. "Everybody knows that when you fall from a great height you never feel it when you hit bottom. You're already dead, probably."

"Is that right?" Mr. Higgins said.

"I looked it up," she said.

"Well it's wrong," he said. "Cause this Indian was wide awake." Mr. Higgins paused. "That Indian didn't scream cause he knew nobody could do a damn thing. Why do we scream for help? So someone will help us. But that Indian was wise and he knew nothing could help him. So he fell silently. He didn't scream because he knew he was going to die."

Jessica looked at me. I tried to swallow the bile in my chest. Had he really been awake? And if so, did he maybe look at the last second at his shoes, and have a fleeting memory of me kneeling behind him?

"I don't think that would work in our book," I said, but thought, Was I the last thing, the very last thing, that crossed his mind? "Cause he's not going to die. He's going to just about reach bottom and then remember that he can do anything he wants. He's . . ." I lost my breath, my sentence, my whole train of thought. I felt like it was me, then, who was spiraling out of control, heading for the hard earth.

"He's gonna swoop back up in the air," Jessica said defiantly. She stood up, walked slowly around the room, stood behind her grandfather's chair and stared at me. "He's going to realize he can fly. He going to save that plane before it crashes."

"That's why it's a comic book," Mr. Higgins said.

On the last day of school, the night of our graduation into junior high, Jessica and I were walking home when we saw Dennis Zeller's mother out walking his dog. We hid behind a bush, watched them walk past us. The dog limped along; he only had half of one of his ears. Mrs. Zeller wore a lot of makeup and smoked while she walked. As she passed us, we heard her whistling.

"She doesn't care that he's dead," Jessica said. "Whistling like that."

"Sure she cares," I said.

"He was a bad kid. How do you think he acted at home?"

I thought of Dennis's voice, rising from the back row and moving through me. I ran to catch up with Jessica.

"When I went back up," I said, "to untie his shoes, he was looking at me."

"No he wasn't," she said. "He was dead."

"But he was looking at me," I said.

She swung her backpack around her shoulder and eyed me coldly. "You're a baby, Alex," she said. "A real baby, you know that?"

"You pushed him," I said. "You're the one who pushed him."

"He wouldn't of fallen if you hadn't tied his shoes," she said. We had reached her front yard and she stood there, glaring. "Let's just forget it," she said. "Please. Let's go draw."

"You were the last one to touch him," I said. "He died because of you."

She hit me in the face, caught me off guard. I landed on the lawn on my butt and put my hand to my mouth, felt warm blood seep through my fingers. I scrambled up to my knees and grabbed her around the waist, pressed my head against her stomach and wrestled her to the grass. I took her by the hair and tried to bang her head into the wet lawn, but she clawed at my face with her hands, scratching at my eyes, my nose, and I kept losing my grip on her.

And then Mr. Higgins was there, his wheels in my face, his strong hand on the back of my shirt. He lifted me off Jessica and I fell backward, covered my face with my hands.

"Why are you trying to kill each other?" he said. "You don't have to kill each other. You don't have to do this."

Jessica sat up. Her hair was caked with dirt. She spit at me. "Bastard," she said. "You baby."

I got up and ran, ran down the street hard toward my house. Running up the lawn I saw Mrs. Zeller standing on the sidewalk down the street with the mangy dog, looking at me.

I tried to talk my parents into letting me skip the sixth-grade graduation. My lip was split and I had a Band-Aid across the bridge of my nose, but they said it was the most important night of the year and I should go no matter what. Jessica wouldn't look at me. She sat in the front row of students and stared straight ahead, not blinking. It reminded me of the night at camp. It was the same look.

Dennis Zeller's parents were the special guests for the graduation. They sat in a roped-off section right below the stage, next to the principal. His mother wore a fancy dress and she still had too much makeup on, more than any of the other mothers. His father had a beard and wore an old suit. As each one of us crossed the stage, Dennis's parents clapped wildly, and then, at the bottom of the ramp, we had to shake hands with the principal and then with the Zellers. I did it, was one of the first ones. I didn't even look up, just held the rolled-up paper in my fist and tried not to think of him, even when his father's sweaty hand held on to mine for what seemed like an eternity. I sat back down in my seat and waited for Jessica's name to be called.

When the vice-principal said her name, I thought at first that Jessica wasn't even going to get up. I watched the back of her head and she seemed not to be moving. I looked out into the audience and caught sight of Mr. Higgins, straining his neck to get a better view from the back where he sat, his wheels locked in place. Then slowly Jessica rose out of her chair. Her eye was black and she had a bandage on her forehead. She walked slowly across the stage, in a daze. When she reached the bottom of the ramp, and let Mrs. Zeller take her hand, she looked up at me. I knew then that I would ride my bike alone that summer, watch television in my empty house. I knew that we would never finish our comic book, that our hero would always be as he was in the last frame of the first issue: inches from the ground, forever unable to remember whether he could fly or not. I sat there and continued to watch as my classmates one by one crossed the stage, smiling like real children, strangers who only cared that tomorrow when they woke up it would be summer, another summer of fun and freedom, and days when the light lasted long into the night.

THE ROCKS
OVER KYBURZ

RAY was sinking, drowning in the yellow light and the screaming of the trumpets aimed at his head. The crowd was a blue and white nightmare, a stark, brilliant vision that transformed the vast high school stadium into a tight box around him. He watched the line in front of him move to the left, then to the right, then forward, marching toward him like an army. He was afraid of them, wanted to drop the baton, turn and run in the other direction.

Later, sitting on the front steps of his house with his wife, the buzz in his head just beginning to fade, he told her he didn't think he could finish the season.

"You say that every year," Wendy said. "Every opening night. It gets better. You get used to it."

"Not this time," he said, stubbing out his cigarette on the concrete step, leaving another black stain among many. "No way. I'll quit, teach private lessons."

She ignored this. "Did you get to talk to Murray after the game?"

He shook his head.

"You would have thought he'd won it himself. Gets a first down on his only carry and there are stars in his eyes."

"It'll wear off," Ray said. "Like everything he does. By Halloween he'll want to take up bobsledding, train for the Olympics."

"Tell him congratulations anyway," she said. She squeezed his thigh gently and he shivered. It was nearly midnight and the streets were quiet, although the twins, Murray and Wes, were still out somewhere, celebrating the victory. "You can't make enough doing lessons," she said. "You know that. You don't have to do the band anymore, but lessons isn't going to cut it. All the woodwinds in town won't carry the house payment."

"Screw the house payment," he said. He stood suddenly, letting her hand fall, and faced the house like an enemy. "We've been here too long," he said. "We said we'd never stay in one place longer than two years. We've been here almost ten."

"We didn't have kids when we said that," she said. "We were probably stoned at the time and planning to string beads for the rest of our lives." She smiled the wistful smile that people take on when they talk about the age of believing in their own immortality, and Ray had to turn his eyes away.

He kicked the step and thought of college, a million years before, when he had played his alto sax in a jazz band in the local bars, when Wendy would come to every show and sit at the table at the corner of the stage, smoking and eyeing him coolly, letting him know that she was his.

"It's late," she said. "I wonder where they could be?"

"They're kids," he said. "They hang out." He gestured toward the house next door. "They took Gretchen out with some of the other kids, probably showing her around town."

"There's so much out there," Wendy said.

"They're probably switching places to confuse her," Ray said. "Like they did to that new art teacher last year. They never get tired of it. That woman got so flustered, she still can't tell them apart. She always thinks they're lying now when they—"

"You should hear some of the stories I hear at school," Wendy said, ignoring him. "Some of the things these kids do, and they're younger than Murray and Wes. You wouldn't believe what goes on."

Ray stopped listening. Ever since Wendy had taken the job as guidance counselor at the junior high a year before she had moments that made him embarrassed for what she had become. Sometimes she kept him up nights talking about peer pressure and drugs and suicide and dysfunctional families. At first he had laughed, thinking she was kidding, playing along for the hell of it. But when it became apparent that she actually believed in some of the things that they had both found hilarious years before he stopped saying anything. He would listen quietly, seething, wondering why she had changed.

"I'm going to bed," he said.

"You don't think we should wait up?"

"Christ, Wendy, they're fifteen years old. We're not approaching daybreak yet." He reached a hand down for her. "Come with me," he said.

"In a little while," she said.

After he got upstairs he went to the bedroom window and looked down on her. She was lazily smoking a cigarette and looking out into the road, waiting. He could love her through this window, he thought, for the rest of his life.

The next morning Ray sat in the screened porch in the back of their house and watched their next-door neighbor, Nancy Wexler, rake leaves. Nancy and her daughter, Gretchen, had moved in a month before, just before the start of the school year. Gretchen was an awkward girl, a year or so younger than Murray and Wes. She played the clarinet in the marching band, held it tightly like a boy with a new shotgun, blew so hard on it that Ray sometimes wanted to laugh at her puffy red cheeks and eyes clenched shut. He drank his coffee slowly. Outside, Nancy was leaning over to push a pile of leaves into a garbage bag. Ray liked to watch her sometimes. She was a small woman, tight instead of loose with age. Most of the time she looked stern, and Ray wondered in a passing way if a good fuck might help. He walked out to the edge of his yard holding his coffee.

"You're to work early," he said.

She looked up, pleasantly for an instant, until, Ray imagined, she remembered her sternness.

"There's a lot to do," she said. "Sitting around isn't going to get these leaves off the yard."

"Makes sense," Ray said. Wendy had told him that the Wexlers had moved away from Gretchen's Iowa farmer father earlier that summer. He wondered if everyone in Iowa was so unpleasant.

"I don't know why I bother," Nancy was saying, giving the bag a kick. "I hear it starts snowing up here in October. I thought California was supposed to be hot all the time."

"Early October," Ray said, smiling. "I guess Kyburz is a little different than Iowa, thank God."

Nancy straightened up and regarded him coldly. She looked as if she were about to say something nasty when the back door of her house slammed and Gretchen came out into the yard with a rake.

"Start over by the oak," Nancy said to her daughter, with a wave to the other side of the yard.

The girl nodded and started off.

"How's the practicing going?" Ray called to her.

Gretchen turned, shrugged a little and blushed. "Okay, I guess," she said.

"Every night for an hour," Nancy said. "And we've been listening to the old Benny Goodman records together."

Gretchen stood awkwardly in the middle of the yard, picking pieces of leaves off the spokes of the rake. Above him, Ray could hear squirrels cracking nuts on the branches of the trees.

"Isn't that right, honey?" Nancy said.

"I'll never be that good," Gretchen said. She looked at Ray for a moment. He thought he saw her roll her eyes before she turned again and began to rake under the oak tree.

"She's going to be quite a musician," Nancy whispered to Ray. "First chair by next year."

"Could be," Ray said.

"Band is her favorite class," Nancy said. She paused. "I played a little in my day, you know," she added.

"Didn't everybody," Ray said. He thought of the number of people who had played "in their day." Like it meant anything. He figured Nancy had probably fiddled around with a flute in the fifth grade, that this gave her some hold over the musical world.

"You watch," Nancy said. "These things are genetic, you know." She leaned down and went back to bagging her leaves, and Ray took thought of his sons, who it seemed would rather do just about anything than sit down to practice an instrument, or listen to a real record.

He went back to the house. In the kitchen Wendy was cracking eggs into a frying pan and whistling quietly.

"What a snot," Ray said. "She's got some crazy stuff in her head."

Wendy stopped whistling and glanced out the window above the sink. "She's not so bad," she said. "What did you say to her? Were you being an asshole?"

"I didn't do a thing," he said. "Just having some friendly neighborly conversation about what a goddamn musical genius of a daughter she has."

"Give her a break," Wendy said, not turning around. "She's had a tough time of it lately."

"Oh, sorry," Ray said. "I didn't know you two had become so close. You counseling her or what?"

"She comes over to talk sometimes," Wendy said. "She's our neighbor. She doesn't know anyone else."

"That farmer in Iowa beat her up or something?"

"Ray," Wendy said. "I don't need your shit today."

"Just curious," he said. "I guess that's all confidential, though. Wouldn't want to risk your professional integrity by talking to your husband."

"Don't start this," she said, looking at the eggs with such intensity that anyone stumbling innocently into the kitchen at

that moment would have thought she was talking to her breakfast. "Go wake the boys, would you? I'm making breakfast."

"It's barely ten," he said. "Let them sleep."

She turned to him, the spatula raised. "I said wake them up,
okay?"

"You're the boss," he said. He climbed the stairs to the boys'
room. Already he was tired, was ready for dusk to fall. He
thought he might take a nap after breakfast. He hoped Wendy
would take the boys shopping or somewhere far away.

The twins shared a room. For two years they had been planning to clean up the basement and make another bedroom out of
it, but they had never been able to come to the decision of who
would get the new room, so they had stayed together on the second floor. They were rarely in there at the same time, anyway.
Football had come to take up most of Murray's time, and Wes
usually went out nights with his friends, a bunch of other serious
fifteen-year-olds who were in all the honors classes.

Wes was the only one in the room. Ray could hear the shower
running down the hall, and was surprised that Murray was already up.

"Wes," Ray said. "Wesley."

Wes groaned and rolled over.

"Get up and get your ass downstairs," Ray said.

Wesley rolled onto his back. "Come on, Dad," he said.

"Don't get pissed at me," Ray said. "It's your mother who's on
the warpath. She's making breakfast and we're all going to appre-
ciate her for it whether we want to or not."

Wesley smiled and put his hands behind his head. "It's awful
early to be fighting, Dad," he said. "She got PMS or what?"

"Something along those lines."

Murray came into the room, a towel wrapped around his
waist. He was a little heavier than Wes, and his hair was slightly
shorter. Aside from that, there wasn't much way to tell them
apart by sight, and often people still confused them.

"You see me last night?" he asked Ray, sitting down on the end
of his bed.

"You looked good," Ray said, although he had been hunting for the trombone part for "When the Saints Go Marching In" at the time and had missed the play.

"Coach slapped me on the butt after the game and said, 'Here's the shit-kicker himself.' Can you believe that?"

"Coach is a wise, wise man," Ray said.

"All right, I know," Murray said. "He's kinda stupid."

"I heard last week he told the boys' health class that masturbating would make their dicks longer," Wes said.

"Shut up, Mr. Band Geek," Murray said. "Jacking off is all the action you're gonna get, all the girls watching you stumble around out on the field with that stupid tuba."

Ray winced. It was his fault that Wes was playing the tuba. He had told him he had to at least march with the band because if he didn't there would only be two tubas, and the letters on the bells of the tubas needed to spell out OWLS. If he had three, Ray had said, he could get away with it, make it OWL. But with only two, he told Wes, the whole school would have a shit fit when they saw the word OW marching out into the middle of the stadium at halftime. So Wes had agreed to suffer through being what he called a "band geek," but only for the season, and only if Ray paid him five dollars a week. Ray did it, but made Wes swear not to tell Murray, or anybody else for that matter.

"I won't be playing for long," Wes told his brother. "This season," he said sourly to Ray, "and that's it."

"Five minutes," Ray said. "You both better be downstairs with smiles on your faces."

Ray closed the door and lingered in the hall for a moment. He was proud of his children, he thought, but not for any particular thing, certainly not for something as meaningless as making a touchdown or getting a good grade. He felt the most satisfaction in just knowing they were becoming real people, getting smarter about things. He knew they were not especially close to each other, that they had different groups of friends, but some nights he heard them talking in whispers in their room and knew that they were forever tied to each other, and to him.

The next Friday was an away game, so there was no halftime show to prepare, just some standard conducting for the pep band, a small group of ten or twelve kids who played at away games to show the team support on foreign territory. Ray was surprised that Wes had asked to come along with the band until he saw him sitting beside Gretchen Wexler, showing her how to wrap herself up in his tuba. They were both laughing, and Ray smiled to himself.

When Murray caught a six-yard pass Ray turned away from his place with the band and saw Wendy and Nancy Wexler rise up out of the stands together. He could barely distinguish Wendy from the rest of the screeching parents, with her blue Owls hat on, her mittened hands clapping. The parents were who he hated the most; more than the kids or the teachers. It was the phony moms and dads who were the worst, beaming from ear to ear every time an Owl crossed into the end zone, their lives beginning and ending with high school football. Every game at least three or four parents came up to him to tell him the band sounded good, or the band sounded weak, or why didn't he try this song or that song, and he wondered that they didn't have anything better to do.

After the game he and Wendy drove home in silence. Wendy watched Kyburz go by out the window, and Ray thought about moving somewhere, maybe to Europe, maybe running off with somebody, the young secretary in the front office, or Nancy Wexler, or even Gretchen Wexler for that matter. Anybody who might be willing to forget her life and travel around the country with him, who would follow him from band to band and bar to bar. He liked to think of this as his main sort of entertainment. While other parents watched football or television or played cards or drank, he liked to sit and think of things he might do, watch the images float by in his head like a memory that hadn't happened yet. Times he would drift off for hours at a time, envisioning a different life.

"I'm going up to the rocks," he said to Wendy as they got out of the car.

"What for?"

"I think I'll play some sax," he said.

"Play here," she said. "Play for me."

"It's quiet up there," he said. "It's easier up there."

He did this every few weeks, take the half-hour hike up the Kyburz mountain, lugging his saxophone case up the trail that began at the edge of their backyard. He hadn't played the sax at home much at all since the boys were young. Before, every December he would bring it up from the basement and play Christmas carols all month, slow and mournful, usually after dinner. The boys would applaud, finger the saxophone, make screeching noises on it until he and Wendy couldn't stand it anymore.

"Don't sit up there smoking pot," Wendy said. "What if some kids go up and see you? We won tonight. They might be crazy enough."

"I'll put it out," he said. "I'll hear them coming."

"I still don't think it's such a good idea," she said.

"Since when?" Ray said. "You used to do it with me."

"Oh, that would look fine now. Kids stumbling over their guidance counselor smoking pot."

"Jesus, Wendy," he said. It seemed to him they kept having the same conversation over and over again. He picked up his sax out of the closet and walked out the back door. The path up the mountain was rough, rocky, and usually slippery. The only time anyone besides him went up to the rocks was on special occasions—big football victories, graduations, times when the teenagers in town got drunk enough to consider making the hike. The draw of the mountain was the rocks, two of them, each about the size of a house, each balanced precariously on one corner on a larger flat rock underneath. Legend had it that there had been four rocks over Kyburz at one time, but that two of them had toppled onto the town sometime before the turn of the century, crushing everything in their path. The best part of the story, Ray had told his boys when they were young, was that the two rocks had not been toppled by a storm, or even a big group of drunken locals shoving with everything they had, but by one person giving the rocks a tap at one particular place. The local teenagers, he knew, stumbled around up there those few times a year, laughing at each other, tapping along the rocks, never seriously considering that one might actually fall and destroy a car or a house that might be their own when it hit the town five hundred yards below. Ray and Wendy had done this too, when the boys were young and still interested in having Sunday picnics at the top of the mountain. Now Ray went alone, playing his saxophone and blowing the smoke from his joint into the cool mist that surrounded everything in Kyburz, even in the summer.

Once he reached the top he sat down on a tree stump to rest and lit a joint. He looked at the saxophone case. There was a time, he was sure, that his instrument actually spoke to him from inside its case, when he would go into his college apartment and it seemed to clamor for attention, like a pet. Now it usually lay still, muttering every once in a while through the leather on nights like this, but mostly content, he imagined, to only be picked up every few weeks. They had grown up together, grown out of certain things. He took a hit from the joint. The sax was quiet. In his mind he saw a hazy picture of his six saxophone players marching around the Astroturf in their uniforms, blowing on their horns some mess that they called music. He looked at the case again. Nothing was stirring, so he lit another joint and thought of Wendy at the bottom of the mountain, dreaming up reassurances she could try out on her weeping seventh graders that would coerce them into believing that whatever it was maybe it wasn't all that bad. He wondered if she had forgotten that those seventh graders would grow up to realize that maybe it was all that bad, after all. He ground out what was left of his joint and put it into his pack of cigarettes, the saxophone case lying still at his side. He picked it up and headed back down toward his house.

On Wednesday night Nancy Wexler came stomping across the driveway to Ray, who was sitting on the front step, whittling away at a walking stick he had found on the trail coming down from the rocks.

"I have a question for you," she said.

He set down his knife and picked up the cigarette resting on the step. "Well?" he said, purposely letting the smoke float out of his mouth as he spoke.

"I'm not so sure that your boys are good for Gretchen," Nancy said.

Ray noticed that Nancy had a mole under her left eye. It looked, he thought, painful.

"What're they doing?"

"That's the problem," Nancy said. "I don't know."

"Sounds dangerous."

Nancy frowned and looked behind Ray through the screen door into the house. "Is your wife home?" she asked.

"Sorry," he said.

"Hear me out," Nancy said. "All right? So the past couple weeks Gretchen starts disappearing with your sons and sometimes doesn't come back for hours. I'm supposed to laugh this off?"

"They're kids," Ray said. "They go off and do kids' things. Gretchen's new around here. They're being nice guys and showing her around. I guess I don't see the problem."

"I swear I heard her come in in the middle of the night last night," Nancy said. "Three hours after she supposedly went to bed."

"The wind," Ray said. "You hear things rattling. Maybe it's the boogeyman."

Nancy bit her lower lip. "I know about you," she said. "I'm not stupid, and I'm not goddamn born again or anything, but I don't think some of the things you do are the best things in the world to be doing around teenage boys."

"Listen," Ray said. "Don't tell me how to live my life and I won't tell you how to live yours." He paused. What he said had sounded lame and he knew it. He imagined himself imagining this scene, pictured the way he would do it if it weren't really happening. "Come on, Nancy," he said. "You're still a good-looking woman. You're still young. You might try doing something exciting yourself every once in a while."

"They're doing something up there on that mountain," Nancy said. Her eyes narrowed. "They're . . . they're smoking pot, is what it is. I'm sure of it. I see them go up there and I've seen you doing it, sitting out on your porch at night as if there were nothing wrong with it."

"I don't smoke pot with my kids," Ray said.

"You can't tell me they don't know you do it."

"I'm telling you I don't smoke pot with them. If you're so worried about it why don't you talk to your daughter?"

"Because I trust my daughter," Nancy said.

"Could've fooled me," Ray said, taking a drag from his cigarette.

Wendy pulled into the driveway with the boys. They had been at the mall and Wendy got out of the car with two big red bags from Macy's.

"Well, hello," she said, coming toward them. She saw the look on Nancy's face and then looked at Ray. The boys took a basketball out of the garage and started shooting around in the driveway.

"What is it?" Wendy asked. She put on the face that Ray knew she put on for her seventh graders. The come-talk-to-me-I'm-the-comforter-and-we-can-work-it-out face. "Is there a problem?"

What Ray didn't need now, he thought, was Wendy pulling this crap. He saw Gretchen come across the Wexlers' yard toward the driveway. Wes passed the basketball to her and it flew past her head.

"Nothing," he said. "No problem."

"I'm sorry to say this," Nancy said. "But you seem like a reasonable person and I think you should know that your boys are smoking marijuana with my daughter."

"They are not," Ray said.

"Oh, Nancy, I don't think so," Wendy said. She shifted the bags from one arm to another. "If you want to talk about it—"

"We've already talked about it," Ray said. "You want to talk to them about it?" He walked toward the driveway, knowing Nancy Wexler wouldn't let him say a word to them.

"Don't you speak to her," Nancy said, following behind him.

Ray took the ball from Murray and let go an arching shot from the edge of the driveway. It bounced off the rim and rolled away.

"You're slippin', Dad," Wes said. "An old man now."

"Hey there, Gretchen," Ray said.

"Hi Mr. Gardner," she said. She looked at her shoes.

"Did you finish the dishes, Gretchen?" Nancy asked, before Ray could say anything.

"Yes, ma'am," Gretchen said. Ray watched her. She was like her mother, he could tell. Someday her shyness would be replaced with the bitchiness that Nancy was so proud of. Gretchen was wearing a big Iowa State sweatshirt that hung off her left shoulder. He looked at the shoulder, the smoothness of it.

"Heads up," Wes yelled. Ray turned and caught the ball coming toward him. He dribbled a few times, then passed it to Murray.

Wendy called to him from the front porch. "Come help me put this stuff away," she said. Ray smiled at Nancy and walked back to the house.

"What was that all about?" Wendy asked, when they were inside.

"She's crazy," Ray said. "She's worried about her little baby girl."

"Do you think they really are smoking pot with her?"

"No," Ray said. He took the bags from her and set them on the stairs, then sat down himself. "They're not smoking pot. Quit worrying about it."

"A lot of kids are smoking pot," Wendy said.

"So what if they are?" Ray said. "Is it the worst thing in the world if they go up on the mountain every once in a while and smoke a joint? What's gotten into you?"

"They're fifteen," Wendy said.

"Last year you wouldn't have cared, and last year they were fourteen," Ray said.

"This is a scary age," Wendy said.

"A scary age? What isn't a scary age? For Christ sakes . . ." He trailed off. Outside he could hear the boys yelling: "He breaks to the left, to the right . . ."

He took her arm again and pulled her down onto the stairs next to him. "Kids go through all sorts of shit," he said. "They're not going to turn into mass murderers just because we don't hover. We need to worry about us, too, you know?" He kissed her on the cheek, then on the chin, then on the neck.

"Ray, please," she said. "I'm worried."

"You're obsessed," he said, standing up. "Everything was fine before you turned into the goddamn queen of insight and sympathy, before you started chumming around with Broom Hilda next door."

Outside the sounds died down in the driveway. Ray went to the door and saw the boys standing in the driveway with Gretchen Wexler between them. They were huddled together, laughing about something. Ray saw Murray point back to the house in a casual way, smiling all the time. Behind them, Nancy Wexler stood in her front yard with her hands on her hips, looking not at the kids but past them to where Ray was standing at the front door. He instinctively ducked back, ashamed to be caught spying.

"They're kids," he said, in answer to something Wendy hadn't said.

The next night he was awake, staring up at the ceiling, when he heard the back door shut. He went to the window and saw that the boys were throwing gravel at the back of the Wexlers' house. A moment later Gretchen Wexler appeared, dressed in sweats. She had a bow in her hair. He watched the three of them start up the trail to the mountain.

Behind him, Wendy rolled over. He turned to her, saw her stretch her arm out to his side of the bed. He wondered for a moment if she still loved him. Then he put on some shorts and left the house.

The night was cold, but Ray was halfway up the mountain before the cold sunk in and he realized he was underdressed. He made it to the top of the mountain before he heard anything; one of the boys, he couldn't tell which, was saying something. He shivered and peered from behind one of the rocks but he couldn't see anyone. There was a crevice between the two rocks, a grassy patch about twenty feet wide, and he figured that was where the sound was coming from. He imagined what he would do if he saw the three of them in there, sitting cross-legged on the ground, passing a joint around. What was he going to do? Take them down to the house and spank them? He smiled and started back down the mountain.

Then he heard a moan. He stopped. The hair on his chest was prickling and all he could think was that he had to get back to the house, back to his warm bed, his warm sleeping wife.

"Hurry up," he heard one of the boys say, loudly.

He turned back to the rocks, crept around the closest one, and slid softly up to the edge of it. He peered between the two rocks, to the grassy patch. Murray was standing naked above Wes and Gretchen, watching. Wes was on top of the girl, and Ray watched his son go up and down, up and down, his young back slick with sweat. Underneath him Ray could only see Gretchen's feet. They were not struggling feet; they were pushing her body into his.

"Hurry up," Murray said again. Ray looked at him. He had an erection, was bobbing up and down on his toes anxiously. "Come on, you guys," he said. "Any day now."

Ray turned away and heard Wesley's breath come faster, heard Gretchen Wexler make some odd noise. Afterward there was a moment of quiet, then he heard Wes mutter, "All right, all right, hold on just a second. . . ." There was a shuffle of leaves, something that sounded like Murray's laugh, then Ray heard Gretchen say, "Hey there, Mr. Football . . ."

Ray staggered backward and stopped in front of one of the rocks. His body felt strangely heavy, and he leaned his back against the rock. It was steady, he thought. Nothing, not even God himself, could move this rock. He looked down toward his house and saw a light on on the second floor.

He stumbled down the mountain, falling twice on the gravel and skinning the heels of his hands. When he had almost reached the bottom he saw the light from his bedroom go off again.

When he got upstairs, she was in bed. He closed the door softly. "Wendy?" he whispered. "Wendy?"

She didn't respond. He felt a sinking feeling that started in his head and ended in puddles under his feet. He imagined she was dead, that they both were dead, that the only thing alive was up on the mountain, in the dark above their home. He took off his shorts and climbed in next to her. She was on her side, facing away from him, and he pushed himself against her back, burying his face in her hair. "Wendy," he said again.

She woke up. "What is it?"

He pushed against her again, harder, and put his arm around her waist. "Wendy," he said. "I love you." It sounded fake, but it was all he could think to say. He thought of the boys, of the fire of being fifteen. "Please . . ." he whispered.

"Where were you?" Her words were slurred; she was barely awake.

"Nowhere."

"The boys?"

"They're asleep. I just looked in on them." He stroked her back with his index finger, from her left shoulder to her right, then back again.

"Ray, please." She sighed. "It's late," she said, burying her face into her pillow. In a moment he could hear her sleeping again.

He got out of bed and went to the window. He stood naked, looking up at the mountain. He imagined that perhaps Nancy Wexler was next door, doing the same thing. He would go to her tomorrow, apologize, be sincere about it. He would say it was nothing. He would believe it himself. And then he would wait at the window for the steadiest thing he knew to shift free of its roots and roll blindly toward all of them.

THE MEASURE OF

DEVOTION

I T was the hottest part of the day in Gettysburg, just past one
o'clock. It was the hour when the ailing General Lee would have
steered his horse through fields of men with heads and hearts
burst open, searching for some bit of shade to sit down in and
catch his breath, gather his thoughts, envision a brighter ending
to this battle than the one that was nearly upon him. I looked up
from my desk, out the window, across the street and into the
cemetery; the heat kept the crowds down a little, but it was mid-
August, nearing the end of the tourist season, so the park was
still crowded. This was my seventh and last summer as an auto-
tour guide at the Battlefield. Twice a day I slid behind the wheel
of an unfamiliar car with people I had never laid eyes on before
and never would again, drove them along the eighteen-mile
tour, pointing to places where men fought and fell, snapping
family pictures at monuments, recounting the highlights of the
great battle. In the fall I'd be moved up to a desk job, supervising
the guides and overseeing some operations at the park. I was glad
for the promotion, but a little sorry too. I'd found that when
you're in a person's car it's not so different from being in their
home—you're the guest, so they try to be on their best behavior,
bending over backward to make you feel comfortable. It was as

little like work as any job out there, probably, especially when you'd been doing it as long as I had. But the new job meant more money, which meant a chance to finally do some work on the old farmhouse where I lived with my wife and my daughter and a baby boy who—though I didn't know about him yet—was curled inside my wife's belly, about the size of a raindrop.

The last time I'd seen Mrs. Spencer was the night her daughter left Gettysburg for points unknown, but twelve years hadn't laid a finger on her. I was sitting there looking out the window thinking about General Lee and I caught her out of the corner of my eye; she's the kind of woman you can't help but see, no matter which way you're looking. She came strolling into the auto tour office with two little boys straggling along behind her like a couple of worn-out dogs. Her eyes were heavy with green shadow the color of Certs, and she was wearing a black skirt that should have been a foot too short for a woman her age, but her legs told a different story. She took one look at me in my Pennsylvania Parks uniform and without letting a beat go by said, "David Peabody, I knew something fine was going to come of you."

"Hello Mrs. Spencer," I said, trying to bend my lips into a smile.

Mrs. Spencer looked at the girl behind the information desk—Sandy's her name—and said, "Will you listen to him? All grown up and he still calls me 'Mrs. Spencer.' "

"He's a honey," Sandy said.

"Of course he is," Mrs. Spencer agreed. She brought her eyes up to mine. "David, please, call me Carolyn. You'll break my heart if you don't."

I stood, opened my mouth to speak, but before I could she was kneeling down at eye level with those two boys, saying, "This here is the man that should have been your daddy."

I was stunned, though I shouldn't have been. It was just like her to come out with something so ill mannered before I could get so much as a word in, try to get a leg up before I'd even had the chance to catch my breath. Both the Spencer women had a knack for that, knocking the wind out of you with just a handful of words. When I was sixteen and it was Gwen throwing me curves I didn't mind, liked it even. But with Mrs. Spencer it was always laced with a dose of malice.

The older boy, who looked to be about eight, took a long look at me and frowned.

"You know my mom?"

"I knew her a long time ago," I said. "I used to live down the block from your grammaw."

"They were high school sweeties," Mrs. Spencer said. This was an outright lie, but for all I knew poor Mrs. Spencer had really led herself to believe it after all these years. She stood up. "We've come for the auto tour," she said. "Don't suppose we might be lucky enough to snag you as our guide?"

I paused. It would have been easy enough to fink out of it; as senior auto guide, I could assign customers to whoever I wanted. But in seven years I'd never dumped a drive on someone else—it just wasn't in my nature.

"Sure thing," I said.

"Thirty-five even," Sandy said, writing up a slip for Mrs. Spencer.

"A bargain," she said, snapping open her purse. "A bargain for a man like David."

Mrs. Spencer had a big '86 Oldsmobile the color of mud. The backseat was littered with coloring books and melting crayons and Tootsie Roll wrappers, and the whole car reeked of cigarettes. Mrs. Spencer lit one up as soon as we rolled out of the parking lot and headed toward the first point on the tour. She held out her pack of menthols to me and I shook my head.

"Naturally," she said, placing them on the dashboard. "Clean as a whistle. I bet you won't even drink a beer."

"I drink a beer now and then."

"Now and then," she said, laughing her way into a death rattle cough. "You hear that, boys? Now and then."

The kids didn't say anything. We drove in silence for a few minutes as Mrs. Spencer puffed on her menthol, and I tried to put everything out of my mind except the four bloody days of the war that were cause for my employment. The ghost of Gwen Spencer had coated me like flop sweat for a full year after she left town, but that was ancient history now, and I was damned if I was going to let Mrs. Spencer make it any more than that.

"We're coming up on our first point here," I said, shifting into my guide voice and slowing the car down to eleven miles an hour without even thinking about it. "McPherson Ridge is the spot where the great battle began, early in the morning of July 1, 1863, when the Union Cavalry first confronted the eastward-heading Confederate infantry."

"You're so educated, David," Mrs. Spencer said. "You should be teaching at the college."

"I don't think they let you teach college if you didn't go to college." I meant it as a joke, but it came out sounding as ugly as something she'd say, and I scolded myself for it.

"Even so," she said. "It's their loss." She took a long pull on her menthol. "Aren't you even going to ask me about Gwen?"

I gripped the steering wheel a little tighter to keep myself grinning. "Alrighty," I said. "How's Gwen?"

"Well, she's left the children with me for the month, if that gives you any idea. The older one is Jeremy and the younger one is Sam. They both have different fathers. Gwen is in Mexico now with the new man."

"Kip," one of the kids piped up from the back.

Mrs. Spencer humphed. "Kip," she said. "You believe that? What in blazes kind of name is that?"

"It's Indian," the younger kid, Sam, said.

Mrs. Spencer ignored this. "Kip had some business in Mexico and Gwen wanted to tag along. *Business*, this is what they told me when they dropped the children off last week. I'm sure you can guess what that means." I glanced at her and she raised an eyebrow. "D-r-u-g-s," she spelled quietly.

I turned onto the Ridge, pointed out the window. "You boys see that old barn over there? Right behind that barn was where the fighting started."

"What was they fighting about?" Sam asked.

"Lots of things," I said. "One reason was that the Southerners wanted to own slaves and the people in the North thought owning slaves was wrong."

Sam leaned forward and rested his chin on the front seat next to my shoulder. He was a runt of a kid, maybe five or six, short and still full of baby fat. Unlike his older brother, he had a sweet and peaceful face, the face of a boy just woken up. "What're slaves?" he asked.

"Black people," Mrs. Spencer said.

"Like Michael Jordan," Jeremy said.

Mrs. Spencer chuckled. "That's right. And that mechanic your mother dated in North Carolina."

"What did slaves do?" Sam asked.

"They did everything," Mrs. Spencer said. "They cooked and cleaned and washed clothes. They did all the chores."

The boys were both quiet for a moment. Then Sam said, "Nana, can I have a slave?"

Mrs. Spencer whirled around. "You most certainly may not."

"How come?"

"Because it's against the law," Mrs. Spencer said. She turned around and faced forward, ground out her cigarette in the overflowing ashtray, knocking several butts onto my boots. "You can see, David, how these children have been brought up."

"Well, they're kids," I said. "They don't know any better."

She sighed. "I suppose you have a houseful of little geniuses by now."

"Just one."

"Does she live with you?"

"Sure she lives with me."

"And your wife?"

"Yep," I said. "She lives with me too."

"Well happy days all around," she said. "Of course you'll pardon me if I'm a little disappointed. You know I always hoped you and Gwen would end up together."

"I know, Mrs. Spencer. I know you did."

"Christ on the cross, call me Carolyn," she said. "You're not in high school anymore." Then she turned full around to address the children. "David loved your mother dearly. He would have married her in a heartbeat. But your mother was a fool even then. She didn't know a good thing when she saw it, did she David?"

I thought it was rude, talking about these things in front of Gwen's little boys. "We wanted different things, your mom and me," I said, looking in the rearview mirror at them, shrugging to show it was no big deal. "That's the way it goes sometimes."

Mrs. Spencer gave a little snort. "You just keep telling yourself that," she said, "if that's what it takes."

"What what takes?" I asked, immediately wishing the words back, practically hearing the land mine triggered under my feet.

"You know what I'm talking about," she said coyly. "We all have to tell ourselves happy stories to keep from putting pistols in our mouths, don't we?"

"You guys like baseball?" I asked, my voice coming out like I had a bone stuck in my windpipe. "You guys follow the O's?"

"I like catchers," Sam said. "They get to wear stuff."

"Baseball sucks," Jeremy said.

"She hasn't changed a bit," Mrs. Spencer said. "In case you were wondering. Still going from one no-good man to the next, dragging these children all over creation, drinking enough booze so she can't see straight when she looks herself in the mirror."

"Mrs. Spencer . . ." I pleaded.

"And now . . ." she went on. "Now she's headed for real trouble. Running around Mexico with a drug dealer who treats her like a piece of trash."

"Kip's not a drug dealer," Jeremy said. "He's a painter. He painted a picture of me and Sam at Christmas and we had camels' bodies but our own heads."

"D-r-u-g-s," Mrs. Spencer said.

We were coming up on the Eternal Light Peace Memorial now and I swung the car over onto the shoulder and unlocked the doors, relieved to have a reason to end the conversation.

"What are you doing?" Mrs. Spencer asked.

"I thought you might like a look at the memorial."

"It's beastly out there. I can see just fine from here."

"I wanna go," Sam said.

"Me too," Jeremy said. "The car stinks."

Mrs. Spencer lit another cigarette. "All right, then, you all go on and I'll sit here by myself in the air-conditioning."

I climbed out of the car and took the boys over to the Peace Memorial. There were dozens of people milling around clicking pictures and reading the plaques. Everybody was here with their kids before school started up again.

"What is this thing anyway?" Jeremy asked, chewing on his tongue and eyeing the monument as if he already had some beef with it.

I pointed up to the top of the monument. "Up there's a candle that burns forever," I said. "They built this thing in 1938. Two thousand soldiers, from both sides, came back and dedicated it."

"They didn't want to kill each other no more?" Sam asked.

"They were tired of killing," I said. "They lit the candle as a promise to not have any more war."

"What if the candle blows out?" Jeremy asked.

"Hey, let's blow it out," Sam said, bobbing up and down like he had to pee. "Come on, let's!" He craned his neck back and blew up in the air as hard as he could until he was whistling.

"Give it up, sport," I said, setting my hand on top of his head. "A tornado couldn't blow that thing out."

"Yeah, but what if it did?" Jeremy asked. "*Then* what?"

"What if, what if," I said, and I couldn't help smiling. "Just like your mother."

Jeremy wrinkled his forehead and stared up at me. "My mother was here?" he asked, suspiciously. "When?"

"Long time ago. She and I came up here every so often."

"To make out?"

I laughed, or tried to. "We were just friends."

"Nana said she was your girlfriend," Sam said.

"Nope," I said. "We used to come up here sometimes and watch all the people, try to guess where they were from. Your mom was really good at it. She'd just look at somebody and go 'California,' or whatever, and then the person'd go back to their car and sure enough it'd have a California license plate."

"My dad lives in California," Jeremy said. "You ever been there?"

"I've seen it on TV," I said. It sounded stupid when I said it, like I had never been anywhere at all besides Pennsylvania. But Jeremy didn't seem to notice.

"I might fly there next summer," he said. "My dad said we could play football on the beach."

"Sounds like a good time."

"Better than staying with Nana," he said. "Nana lies in bed all morning and smokes cigarettes and tells me how great her life used to be."

I winced. It was all I could do not to scoop a kid up in each arm and start running as fast as I could, bolt through the woods and break out on to Mummasburg Road, then sprint the mile and a quarter to my house. I could save them, even old mean-spirited Jeremy, I was sure of it. I'd just plunk them down at my kitchen table and start showing them what a real family was like. And the saddest bone inside me believed that, if I was to steal off with those boys, Mrs. Spencer would just drive her big muddy Olds back home, thanking her lucky stars the whole way.

"Your mom'll be back soon," I said. "Won't be much longer."

"How do you know?" Jeremy said. "Last year she left us with Nana for the whole summer."

"Nana said she's shellfish," Sam said.

"Selfish, stupid," Jeremy corrected him. "Not shellfish."

"She ain't either one," I said. "You respect your mom, both of you, no matter what your Nana says. She's a great lady."

"Oh yeah?" Jeremy asked. "What's so great about her?"

I took a deep breath. "You know what she did one time? One time we found a baby squirrel next to a garbage can, all chewn up by some dog, its legs hanging off and its little head all smashed in, but still breathing. She picked up that bloody squirrel without a second thought, took it home and fed it out of an eyedropper until it was better. She let that nasty thing sleep in her bed for a whole month."

"Wow," Sam said, his eyes wide. "What'd she name it?"

I shook my head. "I don't even remember," I said. But I remembered all right; she'd named that crippled squirrel after me, just so every day at school she could drop off-hand remarks like "David couldn't keep his paws off me all night" or "It tickles when David licks my neck," trying to get a rise out of people, make people blush. Then when we were alone she'd laugh and laugh about it, and I'd laugh along, wishing all the while that damn squirrel would hurry up and die or get better because nobody blushed more than me when those things came out of her mouth, and she didn't even notice, just tossed me little winks like I was in on the joke.

"Squirrels carry disease," Jeremy said.

"That's not the point," I said, shaking her winks out of my mind. "The point is, your mother's got a good heart."

"Her heart sucks," Jeremy said. "If you ask me."

I know only pieces of the lives of the men who fought at Gettysburg, but I know their deaths by heart. This ground belongs to them, and I do my best to remember that, no matter how many thousands of tours I've driven. When a passenger starts getting bored, or acts unimpressed, I stop the car, no matter where on the tour we are. Once they've got their feet on the ground I tell them that the very spot they are standing on once held a young man who had a wife and a family and a dog and a favorite meal and a song he loved and that he breathed his last breath where they now stand, that his blood is under their feet. I take my time on the tour, because I know that, for most people, this is their best chance to understand what happened here. But driving along in the Olds, I found my right foot a good bit heavier than usual; I sailed past the North Carolina and Virginia memorials without even easing up on the gas, much less laying on the brake. I skipped over the whole second day of the battle. I left out Pitzer Woods, Warfield Ridge, and thousands of dead soldiers all in the name of speed.

"Hey Nana," Sam said. "David said Mom let a nasty squirrel sleep in her bed for a whole month. Is that true?"

"Your mother's let a lot of nasty things sleep in her bed," Mrs. Spencer said. "Some of them for more than a month."

I laid on the gas, roared past Little Round Top. I was pushing fifty at this point, a speed I would have personally fired any junior guard for, without hesitation.

"I wanna see some guns," Jeremy said from the backseat.

"Yeah!" Sam shouted. "Guns!"

Mrs. Spencer mopped her forehead with a Dunkin' Donuts napkin. "Where are the guns?" she asked wearily.

"Some cannons up ahead," I said. "At the Wheatfield. Not much to see, though."

"I wanna see 'em!" Sam shouted.

I gave in, pulled the car over and the boys shot out of the car one after another like a couple of bullets, bolted across the street without looking and shoved some little girls out of the way to sit on the barrel of the cannon.

"This is the worst summer in years," Mrs. Spencer said, fanning herself with the napkin. "Even with this air blowing it might as well be hell."

"It's not so bad," I said, slanting the blowers her way, wishing she would stop sweating.

"Listen to you," she said. "You never say a disagreeable word about anything, do you? Not even the damn weather." She leaned back in her seat and sighed. "I remember those summers you and Gwen were in high school, you all would lie out on the front lawn under the sprinkler, yapping and yapping all day long. I always wondered how two kids had so much to say to each other."

"Well, that was it," I said. "We were kids. We could talk about anything, didn't matter what it was." I found myself smiling, just a little, and I felt my eyelids droop. Thinking about those days cooled me as good as any breeze ever had: the soft bed of wet grass, the icy water raining down on my bare legs, the sound of Gwen breathing beside me. We'd lie there with our eyes shut, stretched out and baking in the sun, nothing to do but let the day go by.

"You must have had the patience of a saint," she said. "I know she was telling you all about her boyfriends. I used to feel so sorry for you having to listen to that."

"She was my friend," I said, thinking of Gwen's foot resting against mine, her cool, wet toes. "That's what friends do."

Mrs. Spencer raised an eyebrow. "David Peabody," she said. "You can't fool me. I was there, don't forget. I saw the way you looked at her when you thought nobody could see. I'd stand at the kitchen window watching you all and think what a damn fool she was."

"She was no fool," I said, but Mrs. Spencer wasn't listening.

"You're old enough now that I can tell you," she went on. "I was a tiny bit jealous, standing there scrubbing dishes just wishing some man would look at me the way you looked at her."

I didn't know what to say to this. I looked out the window at the boys—they were trying to fit their heads into the mouth of the cannon—and waited for what she'd said to disappear.

"A damn fool," she said again. "Let me tell you . . ." She started whispering, like if she spoke quiet enough she might not hear herself. "When she dropped the boys off last week I saw purple finger marks on her arm, like little grapes. It wasn't the first time, either. And you know what she told me when I asked about them? She told me she bumped into a door. I said I'd never seen any door with fingers, and she said—"

"We should go," I said. "We got a lot of ground to cover yet."

"If I told her once I told her a thousand times," she said, raising her voice, "that boy's your very best friend and he loves you better than any man ever will. Don't you leave that boy behind to follow one of those . . . those—"

"She didn't want to live in Gettysburg for the rest of her life," I said. It came out nearly a shout, and I rubbed my thumbs hard on the steering wheel and stared out over the Wheatfield. "Some weekends, you know, we'd get in the car and just start driving, didn't matter which way. We'd just drive and drive and you should have seen her looking ahead at the horizon, like she wanted to drive right into it."

"So why didn't you just keep driving, David?" she asked. "That was what she wanted, wasn't it?"

"I couldn't just keep driving," I said, although I knew as soon as I heard it come out of my mouth that it wasn't true, that I could have kept driving, that there wasn't anything stopping me but my own self. "We had to get home," I said, my voice ringing falser with each word. "We had stuff to do . . . we had to go to school, right? Our whole lives were here."

"Your life was here." She shook a cigarette from the pack and lit it, blew a cloud of smoke into the windshield. "Her life was anywhere else. She didn't care one whit what anybody else wanted."

"Come on, Mrs. Spencer," I said. "You talk like you two never had a good time together in your lives. I remember one night I came up to the house and I seen you all through the living room window, dancing to some disco song, swinging each other around, laughing your heads off. You want to tell me you don't remember that?"

"I don't remember that."

"Well, you can't blame her for you not remembering."

"She's *my* daughter," Mrs. Spencer said. "I can blame her if I please."

"I need a rest stop," I said. "I'll be back in a minute." I got out of the car and walked over to the small concrete building that held the rest rooms. There was nobody in the men's room, and I stood there at the basin looking at my face in the smudgy mirror and scrubbed my hands with hot water and blue soap until my knuckles were red and my fingers ached from rubbing. I never understood people like Mrs. Spencer, never understood squeezing out the same pain every damn day like water from a sponge and then soaking it up just to squeeze it out again. Who's got time for that, with all the other things there are to do?

Lots of times, especially on afternoon tours, people start getting grumpy by the time we hit the High Water Mark, the second-to-last stop on the tour. They've used up their roll of film and their minds are heavy with the thought of so much killing, and they start wanting me out of the car so they can leave the damn war behind and go to McDonald's. Sometimes I want to say, hey, don't you think the guys who were getting shot at would have liked to call it a day about now, after two hours? But it was me, this time, who was willing to cruise right past the High Water Mark, and Mrs. Spencer who—suddenly all hell-bent on giving the boys a history lesson—said, "Let's get out here. This is important, isn't it, David?"

I stopped the car and Mrs. Spencer opened her door and got out, gave her short skirt a little wave in the air like a bored cheerleader, trying to get some breeze between her legs. I didn't want to get out of the car. I didn't want to follow her anywhere anymore.

"This was the end of the line," I said, shutting the door behind me and swinging the keys around my finger. "This here was as far as they got."

"Who?" Sam asked.

"The Rebels. They made one last charge to try to get over this wall, but the North had better position, picked off the Southern boys one by one as they came across that field. That was the end for them."

"The war was over?" Jeremy asked.

I shook my head. "It went on," I said. "And on and on. But there wasn't no use anymore. The South lost the war right here where you're standing."

"The North was better than the South," Mrs. Spencer explained. "Stronger and smarter. That's why you should always live in the North."

"Where are we from?" Sam asked.

"You were born in Houston, Texas," she said. "And Jeremy was born somewhere in Michigan, God knows where exactly."

Jeremy's eyes lit up. "Hey Sam. I'm North and you're South. I whipped your ass."

Sam burst out crying, big fat baby tears that come from being hot and tired and always on the short end of the stick. Mrs. Spencer turned around and whacked Jeremy on the back of the head hard enough to make him stumble.

"You're both from right here," she said sternly. "You're Pennsylvania people, through and through. Isn't that right, David?"

I ignored her, crouched down and put my hands on Sam's shoulders. "You know what, sport? It doesn't matter where you're from. They're good folks everywhere you go."

"I whipped your sorry ass," Jeremy said again, dancing around behind me, just out of reach of his grandmother's quick hand. "I blew your sorry Southern ass to bits!" There was a real meanness to his voice, not like a kid's at all, but an ugly grown-up meanness so full of malice I felt my fists clench. I might have had it in me to hit him too, if Mrs. Spencer hadn't suddenly let go with a long, high moan that made the hair on my arms stand up.

"You see what I put up with?" she wailed. "Do you see? Fight and cry, fight and cry, all the livelong day." She had gone all white and was sweating like crazy; her cigarette was sticking to her lips. I had only ever seen her like this once before, the six-teenth of August, 1983. We were sitting on her front porch wait-ing for Gwen to come home, and it was getting later and later and Mrs. Spencer started quivering so that the porch swing trem-bled under us, started saying, "She's gone for good this time, David, I can feel it," and I kept saying, "No, no, she'll be home soon, any minute now," knowing it was true because she always came home eventually, and if it was really late and she had a night's full of stories to tell me, she'd show up at my house at two or three in the morning and I'd hear that old car of hers rumbling up the gravel drive and I'd go downstairs and we'd sit until dawn in my parents' basement smoking cigarettes, and she'd tell me all the places she'd go if she only had a way to get there.

"I didn't deserve this life," Mrs. Spencer said. "I know I didn't."

"I wanna go home," Sam said, sucking in a noseful of snot.

"You got no home, stupid," Jeremy said.

I told Mrs. Spencer to drop me at the cemetery across from the visitors' center. I didn't want to go back to the office, didn't want to see anybody. But Mrs. Spencer left the car running with the boys in it and started after me. I tried to outwalk her, but it was no use.

"It's her fault, isn't it?" she asked me, skipping a couple steps to catch up. "We tried to give her a good life, didn't we David?"

"Just let it go," I said, walking quicker. "Please . . ."

She grabbed my arm. "I just want you to say I didn't deserve this."

I spun around and shook my arm from her grasp. "Why is it all about *you*? Don't you ever for one second think about anybody else?"

"What—like Gwen?" she huffed. "Is that it? It's so easy for

you to be devoted to her, isn't it David, that little girl in your mind? Well I don't have that luxury anymore. That little girl is dead to me; I got those boys in the car as a reminder of just how dead she is."

"And what about those boys?" I asked. "You ever stop to feel bad for them? You ever think about what they might be feeling?"

She opened her mouth, then closed it.

"You don't, do you? All you can see is what's been done to *you*, how *you* been hurt, how *you* didn't deserve this."

She puffed up all haughty like a peacock. "I'm no different from anybody else."

"Wrong," I said. "You're different from *me*. You don't see me being spiteful, do you? You don't see me blaming. Tell me something—you really think Gwen deserved the life *she* got?"

She took a deep breath in. "Some days I do," she whispered, and her voice shook from the truth of it. "Some days when I'm really low I think she got what she deserved, men who treat her like trash, a life of always waking up in a new place, never knowing where she's gonna be at the end of the day." She paused, let her breath out slow and deflated right there in front of me. "But she's still my little girl," she said. "So I keep on taking these boys whenever she asks, and I keep on mailing her checks even though I know the money's up to no good, and I keep on bailing her out of one calamity after the next." She reached out and touched the tips of my fingers. It was the gentlest thing I'd ever seen her do.

"I've presumed too much," she said. "You're a fine man and you always have been. Too fine for the likes of an old shrew like me."

She walked away then, back to her brown Olds and those doomed little boys and her menthol cigarettes, and I stood there with my toe against the memorial, wishing her the very worst I'd ever wished on anybody. *Bitch*, I heard myself whisper, and I felt a sudden and furious grief wash over me. It was something I had not felt the likes of in a dozen years, not since I was a boy of seventeen and lying in bed in my room in my parents' house on a humid August night. Lying there naked and damp with sweat, I had no notion that I would someday recover, no hint of future grace. I couldn't know that I would one day have a beautiful wife, children, a house of my own. All I knew for certain was that I would surely splinter and die if I didn't hear that car rumbling up the gravel drive. And I tried not to think about where I knew she was, in the passenger seat of a car driven by a boy who must have been braver and wiser and more alive than I could ever be. I tried not to think of her bare feet hanging out the window, or her blond hair in the wind, or of the places she was going without me. I just lay there dying all night long while she was getting farther and farther away.

"She got what she deserved," I whispered. Nobody was there; nobody heard me, so this time Abe Lincoln had it right. *The world will little note nor long remember what we say here,* he had told the crowd who was gathered on this field. It was etched in gold letters right there on the plaque in front of me, and it was my only comfort.

SOME SAY
THE WORLD

T H E R E is fire in my heart. I do what I can.

I sleep deep sleep. I sit in my bedroom window, bare feet on the roof, and scratch dry sticks across the slate. In the two months I've been living here, though, I've spent most of my time playing board games with Mr. Arnette, my mother's new husband. He seems to have an unending supply of them in his basement from when his kids lived at home. My mother isn't around very often. She works at the makeup counter at Neiman Marcus, although she really hasn't needed to since she and Mr. Arnette were married. Mr. Arnette retired a few years ago, at forty-five, when he sold the windshield safety glass company he had started right out of high school for what my mother described as "a fancy sum, for something that still shatters." It was right after that that she met and married him. But she works anyway, only now she calls it a hobby.

It's early March; more importantly, Monday night, the night my mother pretends to be in class at community college. This semester it's poetry, but she's run the gamut. Two summers ago she thought she had me convinced she'd taken up diving.

When she comes in the door a little after nine she sets her clearly untouched poetry book on the end table next to where I am on the couch.

"How was it?" Mr. Arnette asks, smacking his gum and not looking up from the board.

"Oh my," my mother says. "You wouldn't believe the things those people wrote then."

"Who'd you do tonight?" I ask her. It is a game that I have worked up. Sometimes I suspect that Mr. Arnette is playing it as well, but other times I think he's just being duped by her. You never can tell with Mr. Arnette. Sometimes I imagine he has a secret life, although he rarely leaves his house. He seems the type of guy who might have boxes of knickknacks buried all over the world for no reason.

"What's that?" my mother asks, separating the lashes over one eye which have been caked with sweat-soaked mascara.

"Who'd you do tonight?" I put a cigarette in my mouth, wait for one of them to light it.

"Oh, Browning," my mother says.

"Which one?" Mr. Arnette asks. He looks up at me, not her, then takes the lighter from his shirt pocket and snaps on the flame in front of my face, so close I could reach out and swallow it.

"Which one?" she asks.

"Which Browning," Mr. Arnette says. The lighter disappears back into his shirt.

My mother misses a beat, then says, "All of them."

She hovers over the Parcheesi board, feigning interest in the game, and her mink stole brushes one of my pieces to the floor. Mr. Arnette makes a disgusted sigh, although it was him, I know, who bought her the thing. She likes to wear it to work, along with a lot of expensive jewelry. She does not work for her customers, she recently explained to me, she works with them.

She pats my head. "About your bedtime," she says, as if I am twelve and have to get up early to catch the school bus, not eighteen and drugged beyond understanding anything much more difficult than Parcheesi and knowing that my mother, at forty, is sneaking around in motel rooms.

•

My parents were divorced when I was five. I have not seen my father since then, but I've been able to keep track of his moods even so. If my mother is irritable on Monday nights I know that my father is considering calling everything off. If she is sad I know that he has asked for her back. If she is her usual perky self, like tonight, I know that things have gone as planned. They have met every Monday in the same motel since I was in the sixth grade and playing with lighters under my covers after bedtime. I used to find motel receipts, not even torn or wadded up, but just lying in the kitchen wastebasket next to orange peels and soggy cigarettes, with "Mr. and Mrs." and then my father's name following. Still, my mother, through eight years and two more husbands, has never spoken of it to me, and acts as if I could not possibly have figured it out. Thus over the years I have been forced to make up my own story of them: passionate but incompatible, my father a dashing and successful salesman, only through town once a week, only able (willing?) to give my mother three hours. Other times I think it is she who insists on being home each Monday by nine, she that likes doling herself out on her terms, only in small doses. I imagine that they do not talk, that their clothes are strewn around the room before there is time to say anything, and back on by the time they catch their breath. It is easier for me to think of it this way, because I can't imagine what they might possibly say to each other.

At Neiman Marcus, where my mother works, they found me in a dressing room last winter with a can of lighter fluid and my pockets stuffed with old underwear and dish towels. This incident was especially distressing because everyone finally thought that after nearly eight years I had been cured, that the fire was gone, that I was no longer a threat to society. The police led me out of the store handcuffed, first through women's lingerie and then smack past the makeup counter, where my mother was halfway pretending not to know me, or to know me just well enough to be interested in what was taking place. They put me away for almost a year for that one, my third time in the hospital since the first fire. The long stay was caused by pure frustration, I'm convinced, on the part of my doctors. The "we'll teach her" philosophy of psychology. Two months ago they let me out, yet again, into a different world where my mother is married, yet again, and I spend my days spitting on dice with her husband and asking politely for matches to light my cigarettes. Either the doctors think I am cured or they have given in, the way I have, the way I did when I was only eleven, when I realized the fire was like blood, water, shelter. Essential.

The thing about fire is this: it is completely yours for one glorious moment. You bear it, you raise it. The first time, in the record store downtown, I stood over it in the bathroom trash can, thinking I would not let it grow, that I would love it only to a point, and then kill it. That is the trick with fire. For that thirty seconds, you have a choice: spit on it, step on it, douse it with a can of Coke. But wait one moment too long, get caught up in its beauty, and it has grown beyond your control. And it is this moment that you live for. The relinquishing. The power passes from you to it. The world opens up, and takes you along. I cried in the record store when the flame rose above my head: not from fear, but from ecstasy.

I sleep sixteen hours a day, more if it's rainy. Another rationale: enough Xanax and I will be too tired to start fires. I am in bed by ten and don't get up till nearly noon. Usually I take a nap before dinner. The rest of the time is game time. It's a murky haze, more often than not. Me forgetting which color I am, what the rules are. Sometimes Mr. Arnette corrects me; other times he lets it go and it is three turns later by the time I realize I have moved my piece the wrong way on a one-way board.

We are on a Parcheesi kick now. Seven or eight games a day. We don't talk much. Mostly we just talk about the game, about the pieces as if they are real people, with spouses and children waiting in some tiny house for them to return from their endless road trip. "In a slump. You're due," Mr. Arnette will say to his men. Sometimes he whispers to the dice. I suspect this is all to entertain me, because he is always checking for my reaction. Usually I smile.

Twice a week Mr. Arnette drives me across town to see my psychiatrist. He reads magazines in the waiting room while I explain to the doctor that I am fine except for the fact that I take so much Xanax I feel my brain has been rewired for a task other than real life. The doctor always nods at this, raising his eyebrows as if I have given him some interesting new information that he will get right on, and then tells me the medication will eventually remedy any "discomfort" I might be feeling. I am used to this, and have learned not to greet with great surprise the fact that no one is going to help me in any way whatsoever.

It's Friday, and on the way home from the doctor's we drive by a Lions Club carnival that has set up in a park near Mr. Arnette's house. It is twilight, and my mother will be waiting for us at home, but for some reason Mr. Arnette follows the waving arms of a fat clown and pulls into the carnival parking lot.

"What do you say?" he says. He takes a piece of gum from his pocket and puts it in his mouth.

I look out the window at the carnival. I don't get out much. Grocery stores are monumental at this point, and the sight of all these people milling around, the rides, the games, frightens me. A Ferris wheel directly in front of me is spinning around and around, and it makes me dizzy just watching it.

"I'm kinda tired," I say.

Mr. Arnette chews louder, manipulates the gum into actually sounding frustrated.

"I think it'd be good for you," he says. He has never said such a thing before, but instead of causing me to feel loved and comforted it makes me nauseous. I've been told everything from shock treatments to making lanyards would be "good for me," in practically this same tone.

I feel like crying, and know if I do that he will panic and take me home. But I don't have the time. He is out of the car before I can well up any tears, and I continue to sit, my seat belt still on, staring out the window into the gray sky. Mr. Arnette stands in front of the fender, gesturing for me to join him.

The last time I was at a carnival was the Freshman Carnival at my high school, five thousand years ago. I went on a Saturday night with a boy named David who took pictures for the school paper. He held my hand as we walked through the crowds of people and he was sweaty—greasy, almost. He stuck his tongue in my ear in the Haunted House ride and I barely noticed because they had a burning effigy of our rival school's mascot on the wall. The fire licked along the walls and I realized with absolute glee that they had set up one hell of a fire hazard.

Mr. Arnette gets back into the car with a sigh, but does not drive away.

"You need to get out more," he says, and I wonder what has changed, wonder if he had a fight with my mother, or sex with my mother, or some other unlikely thing.

"Used to take the kids here," he says, spinning his keys around his finger. I don't even know his kids' names. They call occasionally, but he speaks so rarely when he's on the phone with them that I can't pick up very much information. I imagine them jabbering away somewhere about work and weather and the price of ground round while he sits on the kitchen stool, picking his fingernails and nodding into the phone.

"I'm not exactly a kid," I say.

"You don't like carnivals?"

"I just don't feel like it."

"If she doesn't feel like it then she doesn't feel like it," he says, as if there is someone else in the car, another part of him, maybe, who he is arguing with.

We continue our drive home in silence. When we stop at a red light he says, "Why do you take all that shit if it makes you feel so bad?"

I laugh at him. It is a question so logical that it pegs him for a fool, and I can't believe I'm really sitting here with him.

"It's not quite that simple," I say.

He shrugs, gives it up, continues the drive home. He is not a fighter, not a radical. Once I came upon him in my bedroom, looking through a photo album of people he had never met. I stood in the doorway and watched him for nearly ten minutes, as he smiled slightly, turning the pages, and I imagined him making up lives for the people in my life. He is that way. Content to not get the whole picture.

I'm standing in the bathroom, trying to stir up enough nerve to just dump them, the whole bottle. My mother taps lightly on the door. I spend more than two minutes in the bathroom and she gets edgy.

"Honey?"

"Just a second," I say. I'm holding them in my hand, all of them. It looks like a million pills, at least, enough to confuse me until I hit menopause.

"Are you sick?"

I close my hand around the pills and open the door just far enough for her to get her foot in it.

"Mother," I say. "I'm fine. I'm just putting on a little makeup."

This gets her, physically sends her back a step. She wants to believe it so much that I can see her talking herself into it.

"But it's almost time for bed," she says.

"Just to see how it looks," I say, giving her a big smile through the crack and inching the door closed again. I hear Mr. Arnette's heavy footsteps come tromping up the stairs.

"What's the fuss?" he asks.

"She's putting on makeup," my mother says in a stage whisper. "Maybe she's trying to look cute for you."

That takes care of my clenched hand. It opens on its own at my mother's words, and the pills sink to the bottom of the toilet, falling to pieces as they go.

"I think she's really just feeling up to it, starting to feel better," I hear my mother say. It is a new tone for her, and this time it's really a whisper, really some sentiment she doesn't want me to hear. I put my ear against the door. "I want her so much to be happy," she says. It makes my chest hurt, she means it so much.

Sunday has come and my eyes can't stay open wide enough. I feel as if I have gotten glasses and a hearing aid over the weekend; colors are brighter and words sharper. No echoes. Words stop when mouths stop. My mother looks at me suspiciously when she comes into the kitchen early in the morning and finds me cooking bacon.

"What's gotten into you?" she asks, pleasantly enough, but with a flicker of panic in her face. Me around the oven means bad news for her. But the heat rising from the burners is only making me warm, and the smell of the bacon is so good that I can't think of much else.

"Just feeling awake," I say.

She smiles, nods, then studies me.

"I'm fine," I tell her.

Mr. Arnette drags into the kitchen, his hair mussed and his robe worn. I have never seen him in the morning.

"Well look who's up," he says. He winks at me.

"Why don't I finish up and you two go in and start a game," my mother says brightly. Mr. Arnette sits down at the table and opens the newspaper.

"I don't feel like it," I say. "Why don't we do something today?"

"We have to go to a party later," my mother says, glancing at Mr. Arnette for support. "I don't think you'd have very much fun there."

I set a plate of eggs and bacon in front of Mr. Arnette.

"Where's mine?" my mother asks.

"You hate eggs," I say.

"We don't have to go to the party," Mr. Arnette says.

My mother frowns, looks from him to me.

"Well I do," she says. "And I think it would be right for you to come with me. She can take care of herself."

I see my mother now, like she has been stripped down out of

her clothes and her skin and even her bones. Her soul is steamed over and dripping fat droplets.

"You all go on," I say. "I don't mind."

I spend the day with my father. I sit out on the porch with the old photo album. The pictures make sense now, fit into an order I have never seen before. My father as a young man raises a tennis racket over his head. He is swinging at something; a butterfly or a bug, though, not a ball. In another he stares away into the distance while my mother pulls his arm, trying to get him to look at the camera. They are so clear now, my father and his bird nose. In one picture he holds me on his lap. I am crying, screaming, and my father is looking at me perplexed. He is barely twenty, I know, and cannot believe that I am his.

My mother and Mr. Arnette do not come home until late. I've lost track of time, still sitting with the photo album when the headlights swim into the driveway. They get out of the car and my mother takes Mr. Arnette's hand, swings it wildly around.

"Oh, darling," my mother exclaims. I am not sure if it is to me or Mr. Arnette.

They are both drunk. My mother stumbles going through the door and Mr. Arnette catches her, leads her inside. Then he comes back out and sits with a grunt on the porch step.

"What have you been doing all night?" he asks.

"Looking through this," I say, holding up the album.

He is quiet for a moment. Then he says, "You ever see your father?" He says it almost as an afterthought, to something that wasn't ever said. He says it like we've been on the porch together all night, discussing my father for hours like he was really one of the family.

"Just in here," I say.

"Think he's still a good-looking guy?"

"Dashing, I imagine," I say.

He snorts out a laugh.

"Why'd you marry her?" I hear myself ask.

He leans back, rests his head on the wood inches from my feet.

"Company," he says. He yawns. And I can see him now too. Safety glass that still shatters. He begins to snore.

"Mr. Arnette?" I say. I reach down and just barely touch the top of his head. He doesn't move.

I go into the house and up the stairs. Their bedroom door is closed, and I imagine my mother is in about the same shape he is, but that they will sleep it off in different places, with dreams of different people's arms.

When I open my door, my mother is standing in my room, the empty bottle of Xanax in one hand, the other hand palm up, as if she were questioning someone even before I arrived.

"Wait a minute," I say. "Just wait."

"I knew it," she says. "I knew there was something wrong."

"Nothing's wrong," I say. "What are you doing in my room? You scared me, standing there like that."

Her mouth opens. "I scared you?"

"I don't think I need those anymore," I say.

"Forgive me if I find it difficult to trust your judgment," she says.

I want a cigarette bad. I had to go all night without them. I go to my dresser and take one from the pack.

"A light," I say. "Do you have a light?"

"Not on your life," she says.

"I'm fine," I say. I accidentally break the cigarette between my fingers and reach for another one.

She sits down on the bed. "You hurt people," she says quietly. "Not just me. You think you take those pills because I don't want you to hurt me?"

"I never hurt anybody," I say.

"You are so lucky," she says. "You could have killed both of us five times over. In that dressing room, did you ever think about the woman in the next one?"

"I wasn't trying to hurt anybody," I say. "You don't understand."

"You're right about that," she says. She sets the empty bottle on the bed and stands up. "I'm sorry," she says. "I can only live with this for so long."

She leaves. I hear her bedroom door close. The house is silent. Below me, Mr. Arnette sleeps on the porch.

I sit down on the bed. I am crazy, all right. I have always been crazy. I see my mother standing on the front porch as I get out of my first police car, only fourteen, braces squeezing my teeth. She stares at me in disbelief when the police tell her that I have caused over a thousand dollars in damage at the record store, a thousand dollars with only one match. It is then that she begins to look at me like a stranger.

It's Monday again, and she is in her bedroom preparing. Mr. Arnette sits in the rocking chair watching a basketball game. I am on the couch. Cheers from the crowd.

"She wants you to go back into the hospital," he says. He doesn't look at me. He moves his glasses from hand to hand.

"I know," I say. "It's okay. Not so bad there."

"Anybody play Parcheesi?"

A man on the court has lost his contact lens. Players are on their knees, hunting.

"Cards mostly," I say. "Lots of jigsaw puzzles."

He nods. "You take those drugs today?"

"No," I say. "Soon enough. It's funny, being able to see so well. But not great so much."

My mother comes into the room and picks up her purse. "Have a good game," she says. She kisses Mr. Arnette on the top of the head, presses her lips into his hair for a long time, until he moves away.

"What was that for?" he asks. He really wants to know, I can tell.

"It doesn't have to be for anything, does it?" she says. She smiles at me for a moment, lingers as if she has something to say, then leaves without another word.

Mr. Arnette swings the rocking chair around and faces me. "You don't have to go," he says. "Imagine me here, all by myself."

"You'll do okay," I say. "Come visit."

He nods, picks up the poetry book from the coffee table, absently flips through it.

"She didn't even think to take it along," he says.

"She doesn't try so hard anymore," I say. "To fool anybody."

He stops on a page, squints at it, puts on his glasses. "Here's one you'd like," he says, smiling. *"Some say the world will end in fire, others say in ice."* He pauses, looks up at me, raises his eyebrows.

"I'd like to see them," I say. I hear my mother's car start up in the driveway. "Just one time, see them together. Be a fly on the wall."

He closes the book. "Let's both be flies," he says.

It is not a long drive, only a few miles, much too close as far as I am concerned, for something that seems like it must be another world. Mr. Arnette stays a few cars behind her, then drives past the motel after she pulls into the lot. He drives around the block twice, then three times.

"What are you waiting for?" I ask him.

"A reason not to do this," he says. He presses down the accelerator and we speed past the motel again. We drive around the city, looking at closed-down stores, empty streets. We don't talk, act as if we really have nowhere to go. He finally makes his way back by the motel, and this time he pulls into the lot. We park at the far end and walk along the row of empty spaces, toward my mother's car. The motel is nearly empty, but the room next to her car is occupied. The shade on the window is up a couple of inches. Mr. Arnette squats down, then reaches for me.

I close one eye and look inside. The bathroom light is on, the door open, and I can see my mother gingerly applying her eye shadow in front of the mirror. There is a man in the bed, sitting up, yawning. He stretches his skinny arms. He is nearly bald, but has a small mustache under his pointed nose. It is a stranger, no one I have ever seen before.

"He looks a lot different than the pictures," Mr. Arnette whispers.

"It's not him," I say, but as soon as I say this I know that it is him. Mr. Arnette looks at me.

"Sweetheart," he says.

My mother shuts off the bathroom light and I can see her silhouette move to the edge of the bed. She sits down, and touches the man on the chest, running her finger from his throat to his waist. He takes her hand and puts the finger in his mouth. It is like watching shadows. She says something I cannot make out. Is it about me? Of course it isn't.

I shiver in the cold. Mr. Arnette takes off his sweater and sets it around my shoulders.

The man begins to put his clothes on, slowly. Next to me, I hear Mr. Arnette's breath catch.

"What is it?" I whisper. I wonder if he can be jealous, if he cares that much.

He only shakes his head. "Chilling," he whispers.

"What?" I say.

"What happens to people."

They are sitting on the edge of the bed together. My mother fumbles for her purse, takes out a pack of cigarettes, gives one to my father and takes one for herself. She lights them both.

"Where will we go?" Mr. Arnette whispers.

"What?" I say.

They are holding hands on the bed. The shadow of smoke drifts above them, the tiny circles of fire all that lights the room.

"Where will we go?" he says again. I lean in against him. He is warm.

Inside the room it is quiet. Together the man and the woman raise the cigarettes to their mouths. For a moment, the faces of my parents glow in the flames. Then Mr. Arnette takes me by the arm and actually lifts me up off the ground.

"Wait," I say. "Wait." But I don't fight him. I want him to take me away, finally. I have seen enough.

We are three blocks from the motel before he remembers to turn on his headlights.

"Slow down," I say. "You're gonna kill us both." I take out a cigarette and push the car lighter in.

"Jesus Christ," he says. "What would she do then?" For a moment he is insane, so much more than I ever could have hoped to be.

There are lights up ahead. Music. It is the carnival, its last night, in full swing. The car wildly spits up gravel as Mr. Arnette rumbles across the lot. He jumps out of the car, dashes forward a few feet, then turns and slams his fist into the hood. Then he is perfectly still. He looks straight at me, and I am afraid to move. The cigarette lighter clicks out. A father rushes his children into the back of the station wagon next to us, where they look at us through the big back window, mouths open.

I pull the lighter out, touch my fingers close enough to the middle to feel the raw heat. Then I light my cigarette and blow smoke into the windshield. Mr. Arnette watches me. I know now that he will never go back to my mother, will probably never lay eyes on her again. Something about seeing them, even though he knew. Something about seeing them.

He turns and starts walking toward the ticket booth. I get out of the car and follow him, stand behind him smoking while he buys two tickets.

"Ferris wheel," he says, turning to me. He smiles slightly. "None of those puke rides. Slow. Slow rides, tonight."

We get into a car that I'm sure is broken. It swings different than the others, crooked somehow. I start to say something, but a girl with yellow teeth and matching hair closes the bar over us and we are suddenly moving in a great lurch forward.

"Hey, hey!" Mr. Arnette says, squeezing the bar and looking down into the park.

"These things are dangerous," I say.

"Bullshit," he says. "We're safer up here than anywhere else in the world."

We screech to a halt near the top, for the loading of passengers into the cars below us. We swing crookedly over the game booths, and I can see us, crashing down into the middle of the ring toss. So many ways to buy it, so few to stay alive.

"I've always liked the looks of Canada," Mr. Arnette says. He is smiling pleasantly, innocent as the dawn.

We start moving again. The motion is hypnotizing, and I no longer feel sick but only strange, detached.

"Nice night for driving," I hear myself say.

He doesn't answer. He is looking at my hands, which are open, palms up on my lap, as if I am waiting for something on this ride. He reaches into his sweater pocket and takes out his pack of gum. He sets it in my hand, and my fingers close around it.

We swing around again. Below me, I see a circle of teenagers standing around a small bonfire, warming their hands. Sparks pop around them and die in the grass as the flame reaches higher. The Ferris wheel whips us toward it, and then away again, up into the night.